Leveled

A SAINTS OF DENVER NOVELLA

JAY CROWNOVER

WILLIAM MORROW IMPULSE

An Imprint of HarperCollinsPublishers

Excerpt from *Built* copyright © 2016 by Jennifer M. Voorhees.

EPub Edition NOVEMBER 2015 ISBN: 9780062387103
Print Edition ISBN: 9780062387127

10 9 8 7 6 5 4

Dedicated to love . . . however it looks, however it lands, however it happens, however it finds you in all its beautiful, complicated, messy glory. Everyone deserves to love and be loved. Also dedicated to an adorable ginger that I happen to think is the bee's knees and a pretty special kind of guy . . . looking at you, Matt Dellisola. Thanks for being my #1 man-fan . . . and my friend.

Introduction

SURPRISE! IT'S LANDO'S book . . . way earlier than planned!

So here's the thing . . . I needed a bridge between the old and the new. I finished the Marked Men series and couldn't have been prouder of my boys, or my readers, with where we left things. And then I jumped right into working on *Built* (available for pre-order now), which is Sayer and Zeb's story and was supposed to be the first book in the Saints of Denver. It's an amazing book. I also couldn't be more satisfied around how it kicks off the new series, but there was this need for a way to connect the two and that was where *Leveled* came in.

Lando and Dom are the perfect mix of old and new, the perfect combo of then and now, and with switching the publication dates around, it really gave me the opportunity to close all the doors and tie up all the story lines that were left from the Marked Men series. It felt right.

It was a story that poured out and was so sexy and fun to write. These boys are a handful . . . together and separately . . . that is always a treat to bring to life on the page.

Of all our original cast in the Marked Men, none deserved closure and the choice to move on and find love like Orlando did. I was happy to give him this story and there are enough familiar faces in this book making appearances that even though this isn't my typical kind of story, it will make all the fans of the original series really happy, and hopefully any new ones that are picking this book up as their first Jay read.

I hope you enjoy the boys as they battle their way through love and fear and just in case you are wondering, the time frame of this book and pretty much all the Saints of Denver books takes place in that space of time between the end of *Asa* and the epilogue . . . so the six months or so that lead up to the wedding . . . you'll have to read the Marked Men to know what wedding I'm talking about. ;)

Also, before you dive in, I want to say that any liberties taken with police protocol and reinstatement after an injury are my own and done so for the sake of the story. Sometimes the reality of things makes for boring fiction, and the lines need to be bent and tweaked to get the story where it needs to be.

I have nothing but respect and admiration for the men and women that choose to protect and serve and it's an honor to give them a voice and a story in my work.

Success is not final, failure is not fatal: it is the courage to continue that counts.

—WINSTON CHURCHILL

Chapter One

Dominic

LEVELED.

Laid out.

Knocked sideways.

Flattened and collapsed.

Breathless and stunned.

I'd had the proverbial rug yanked out from under me more than once in my twenty-five years. The first time had been when my father's partner showed up at our front door sobbing uncontrollably. Dad had taken a bullet during a routine traffic stop and in the blink of an eye I went from little boy to the man of the house. It was my job to take care of my mom and two younger sisters, so that's what I did.

The second time was when my very best friend in the entire world tapped me to teach her how to kiss when we were just about to enter high school. Royal Hastings was everything a teenage boy should want, beautiful, funny, and sweet as could be with a rack that wouldn't quit. Kissing her should have been a treat and not a chore. I loved her something fierce, so when our lips touched and I was left wholly unaffected and completely unmoved, it forced me to stop and really consider why. That summer when I went away to a very exclusive baseball camp and met a boy named Riley who also wanted to practice kissing, it became crystal clear why touching Royal did nothing for me. I liked boys, really liked them, in a much more than friendly way. Initially, the revelation had freaked me out, sent me scrambling and into denial, but I was too close to my family, too tight with Royal, to keep the revelations quiet for long. And like everything else, I eventually just accepted it was who I was along with being my family's protector and Royal's bff. Being gay was simply another facet of the man I would ultimately become. So it took a backseat, to getting out of high school and doing my late father proud and becoming a cop just like he was.

I managed to reach every goal I set out for myself. I was focused and diligent, often working harder than the next guy because I felt like I had not only a legacy to live up to but also more to prove. When I got shot in the line of duty, which led me to taking a header off of a building, which, of course, did a brutal number on my body, the uncertainty of what my future held as I healed nearly paralyzed me. Lately, I was surly, argumentative, and a general pain in the ass to be around. My family was sick of me, and it had killed me to watch Royal, who was now my partner on the force as well as still being my best friend, nose-dive into a downward spiral of guilt because she felt like my getting hurt was her fault. It was a mess. I was a mess, both physically and mentally.

I always considered my typical recovery time pretty quick when things shifted and tilted around me. I was a man that rallied and adapted to my changing circumstances with a stiff upper lip and practical sensibility. This go-around, I was scrambling. Everything was off-balance, and I couldn't seem to find my footing, no matter how much I fought to remain sturdy and upright. It pissed me off even more that my current disorientation had little to do with the limp left over from my recently shattered leg and my questionable future with the Denver Police Department, and everything to do with the somber-faced man sitting across from me.

It had taken months to get an appointment with him, and that was with Royal pulling strings because she shared mutual friends with the man. I had to wait for an opening in his schedule that was packed because the guy was in demand across the board when it came to complicated athletic injuries. The guy was no joke when it came to fixing broken bodies and he didn't take on just anyone as a client.

He was in demand. He was supposed to be a miracle worker, with magic hands and the perfect touch. He was my last hope that I could get not only my body back in working order but also my place on the force.

Orlando Frederick also happened to be a gorgeous specimen of a man and he unnerved me with the way he kept staring at me intently out of a striking pair of gray-ish blue eyes. He was watching me like I was a complicated math problem that he was trying to solve. I didn't like being dissected and picked apart. I was used to being the one in the position of authority and command. So sitting there silently while my last shot at getting my life back decided if he was going to help me out or not wasn't any fun, and it took every single shred of self-control I had not to fidget or twitch anxiously under that cool, unwavering gaze.

I decided to check him out in a different way than the detached and calculating way he seemed to be analyzing me. He was a redhead. Not a full-on orangey-red ginger, but his auburn hair leaned further on the red side than the brown, and it was cut in a fashionable style that was super short on the sides and much longer on top. He had a paler complexion than I normally found attractive, and he had freckles that dotted the bridge of his nose. Who knew freckles could be so sexy? Rusty eyebrows arched elegantly over eyes the color of a mountain stream and while all of that should have made him seem wholesome and approachable, it had the opposite effect. All of those distinct and elegant features combined made him seem way more refined and sophisticated than the men I typically found myself interested in.

He was dressed in a black polo shirt with his clinic's logo on it and when he stood up to shake my hand, I noticed he was an inch or so taller than me but built along far leaner and longer lines. He was in great shape, I figured he would have to be, considering his job, and he made me feel bulky and clumsy as he guided the way into his office. He seemed like he was built for speed and flash, whereas I was built to take a beating and keep on going. There wasn't a hint of sophistication or refinement about me, and I liked it that way. It made fitting in with the guys on the force slightly easier. They all knew I was gay, but I went out of my way to make it a nonissue.

After an initial question-and-answer session, where he quizzed me about the accident, the subsequent injuries, and what kind of physical therapy I had been doing up to this point, he lapsed into silence, where we just spent a good five minutes staring at one another. I was waiting for him to tell me there was nothing he could do. That's what the doctors said. That's what the physical therapist at the hospital said. That's what the orthopedic surgeon said after my last surgery. I was always going to have a limp, and my shoulder was always going to be stiff, making my movements stiff and hampered. Neither of those things was acceptable when you chased bad guys around for a living.

He reached out and shut the medical file in front of him and leaned back in his chair. His eyebrows arched up, and he laced his fingers together and put his index fingers under his chin.

"What exactly are you after, Mr. Voss?" His voice was smooth and modulated. I was a disaster, a bundle of nerves and anxiety, and this dude was acting like we were talking about the weather, not my entire life and everything I had ever worked my ass off for.

Defiantly I spread my legs apart and slumped back in

the chair across from him, making it a point to affect a posture that was as casual as his was professional. I had on a faded DPD T-shirt and a pair of jeans with a hole in the knee, and both were a little baggy since I'd lost some of my bulk being laid up in the hospital after the accident. If the guy across from me was a cherry-red Ferrari, then I was a rusted-out and battered John Deere tractor in comparison.

"I want my life back, Mr. Frederick. I want to be able to move the way I used to. I want to pass the department physical so I can go back on patrol. I want to be able to walk without needing a crutch or a cane. I want to be the way I was before I got hurt." I was asking for the impossible and I knew it. "And please call me Dom."

He dipped his chin down a little, and the edge of his mouth tilted up in a slight grin. Damn, the man was good-looking. I blew out a breath and lifted up my hands to run them over the top of my shorn hair. I was hanging on to my sanity by a thread and my unexpected reaction to the guy that I was hanging every hope I had left on wasn't helping matters.

"All right, Dom. You can call me Lando. That's what my friends call me."

I felt one of my eyebrows shoot up. "Are we going to be friends?" I didn't mean for it to come out sounding as suggestive as it did, but there was no taking it back once the words breached my lips.

His rust-colored eyebrows dipped down over his nose, and the grin on his mouth pulled downwards in a grimace that I couldn't miss. I had a moment of panic that I might have blown any shot at securing his help by shooting off my big mouth. Nothing like making the guy uncomfortable, especially since he gave zero indication that he liked boys the same way I did. As a man that rarely discussed or broadcasted his sexual orientation, I found that it made it slightly harder for me to be able to instantly gauge whether another man was interested in me the way I was in them. I always played my cards close to my chest. Being a cop was already a hard job. Being a gay cop made the job that much more challenging, so I learned early on that my personal life wasn't a topic of conversation I wanted open for discussion. Like I said, a nonissue.

"No, Dominic, we aren't going to be friends. In fact, you're more than likely going to hate me. You're going to regret walking in this office, and you're going to think I'm the worst person in the world. But I will do my best to get you the results you are after. I'm going to work you hard and in the end you're going to thank me for it."

I opened my mouth to throw out another inappropriate response about him working me any way he wanted to, but I stopped myself just in time. I bit down on the tip of my tongue and nodded my head slowly.

"You think you can fix me?"

He shook his head slightly, and a hank of reddish hair flopped forward and hung in his face. I wanted to reach across the desk and move it out of those cool blue eyes.

Shit. That wasn't good. Mr. Fancy-Pants didn't need me lusting after him, and I didn't need the complication of a hard-on while I worked my way back to 100 percent.

"I think you can fix you. The leg doesn't concern me as

much as the shoulder. I mean it's still pretty bad, and when you dislocated the shoulder, you ripped all those tendons and muscles." He shook his head in sympathy. It had hurt worse than anything I'd ever experienced, and it was refreshing that he wasn't just writing me off as a lost cause. "I know you had reconstructive surgery and that always affects mobility and flexibility. I'm wondering if we can work to make your left hand dominant, so that you don't have to worry about limited movement on the right side."

I blinked at him stupidly and let out the breath I was holding. Why hadn't that ever occurred to me? I was at the gun range two to three times a week trying to get my arm back in shape and frustrated that it was still lagging. Why hadn't I thought to try out my left side?

I cleared my throat. "Uh, okay?" I leaned forward a little and put my hands on my knees. "Does this mean you're going to take me on as a client?"

As I said the words, I couldn't keep the relief and hope I was feeling from flavoring them. I wanted to jump up and grab him in a rib-crushing hug. The only thing stopping me from doing it was the fact that I wasn't exactly in jumping-up condition yet, and I wasn't entirely sure that if I wrapped him up in my arms I would stop at hugging. I hadn't ever had such an overwhelming response to anyone in my life, and it was making me feel unpredictable and off-kilter. I needed to keep myself in check so he could help me, and I could get back on the job.

That was all that mattered. I needed him to save my future, not make out with me.

Something sharp glinted in his crystalline gaze as he

stared at me and suddenly the vibe he was giving off went from detached and clinical to something else, something much more like the distinctly interested vibe I was pretty sure I was giving off.

A half grin pulled at his mouth again, and he moved his hand to push his hair out of his face.

"Yeah, Dominic, I'm going to take you on."

I blinked again and felt my nostrils flare a little bit at the subtle innuendo.

"Uh, okay. Thank you." I lifted a hand, rubbed it across the back of my neck, suddenly nervous and out of sorts for different reasons than the uncertainty surrounding my future.

"You won't be thanking me shortly, but I'm happy to do my best to help an officer injured in the line of duty. I can't make any promises because no matter how hard you try or how badly you want it, the body often has its own agenda and limits. Those limits will win every time, but we can try and I'm optimistic."

Thank fuck. Finally someone besides me that was optimistic.

I curled my hands into fists on the tops of my thighs to keep from reaching out and grabbing him. I wanted to hold on to this man, this stranger, for a lot of reasons, and only a couple of those reasons had anything to do with the long-awaited words he was saying to me.

"It's going to be a lot of work. It's going to hurt. It's going to be frustrating, and the results aren't a guarantee, but I'll be there every step of the way and whether we succeed or fail, we do it as a team. That means you are going to have to trust me and believe that whatever I am asking of you is in your best interest."

My hands tightened even further as I nodded numbly. I was used to being the one that took care of everything. I was used to being the man in charge, the pillar of strength and support, and even though Royal was my partner at work, I still felt like it was my duty to look out for her, not because she was a woman but because she was my closest friend and I couldn't imagine my life without her in it. I'd never really had anyone looking out for me or my best interest before. I wasn't quite sure what to do with it. So I just muttered a weak "okay" and stood to shake his hand when he rose from behind the desk.

There was more than a spark when our palms touched. There was an electrical current that blazed a fiery trail all the way up my injured arm and made my spine tingle at the contact. I held his pale gaze and searched openly for any sign that he felt it, felt something. It was unexplainable and overwhelming, but something was happening between the two of us, and I saw his skin darken slightly and his eyes widen just a fraction. He was better at hiding his response than I was, but I was trained to look for the tiniest changes in expression, and they were there on his handsome face. He was as affected by me as I was by him.

He released my hand and cleared his throat. "I'll see you on Wednesday. We'll go through the paces and see exactly where you're at so we have a baseline to work from. Be ready to sweat."

I couldn't hold back the chuckle or the leer that crossed my face. "I don't mind working up a good sweat."

I could've sworn he blushed, but I didn't intend to push my luck any further, so I told him I would see him Wednesday and headed for the door. I let my gaze skim over all the awards and degrees he had decorating his shelves and took in the pictures he had decorating the space. I was impressed to see him standing with his arm around Peyton Manning and another where he was with Carmelo Anthony when he still played for the Nuggets. Apparently Lando was a hockey guy, because of all the sports stuff he had on the shelves, most of it was dominated by the Avalanche, and there was more than one picture of him with Patrick Roy and with Gabriel Landeskog, proving he was a longtime fan.

Apparently in this line of work he got to live a fan boy's dream, but what really caught my eye was an obviously personal picture that stood out the most amongst the autographed and flashy memorabilia. It was a picture of a much younger Lando standing next to another boy in his late teens who was wearing a high-school football uniform. Lando was smiling ear to ear, arm wrapped around the padded shoulders of the stiff and obviously uncomfortable dark-haired boy. This wasn't a fan excited to meet a ball player. These weren't two buddies excited after a big win. This picture showed a young man proud of his boyfriend. There was obvious affection and pride on the picture of Lando's face. Both boys were so young and so obviously in love, at least it seemed to me. I could also tell there was something captured in that innocent snapshot that made the dark-haired boy uneasy.

Interesting. I couldn't help but wonder if the extraordinarily handsome football player in the photograph was still in the actual picture, as in Orlando's life currently.

All of those wayward thoughts took a backseat to the silent thrill that zapped through my entire body at what I considered irrefutable proof that Mr. Fancy-Pants did indeed like boys the same way I did, and we were about to spend a lot of time getting sweaty together on the regular.

Bring it on.

Chapter Two

Lando

A COP.

A big, burly, and surly protector of the law and innocent.

A warrior and a fighter. A man that would push and push until he broke and then push some more.

A hero.

Dominic Voss was all of those things and so much more. He was the reason that taking on cases for those that served selflessly, for those that gave their lives to be the first line of defense in a world that was full of really terrible things, was something I had to do. I did it in order to balance the scales between making a nice living off the rich and famous, and getting to help people that needed it. I wanted to have purpose. I wanted to help.

I genuinely wanted to repair things that were broken. I wanted to help people stop hurting whenever I could.

For every injured hockey player or football player that came into my clinic, I made sure that the cost of their care and rehab would be enough to cover the rehab of at least two disabled veterans or first responders injured in the line of duty. My loyalty was to the health and well-being of the body, not to the wallet attached to it and how fat it may or may not be. Broken bodies came from all walks of life and I firmly believed if I was able to help, then I would.

The zealous need to heal, the driving desire to bring men and women back to their former glory, came from not being able to save the one broken body I wanted to the most in the world. My therapist had had a field day with me after I came clean about the ugly fight and ultimatum I laid at the feet of my first and only serious boyfriend the night he died. She called it projection. She told me I was blaming myself for the accident even though Remy had been driving too fast for the rainy conditions that night, and as a result I was trying to save *everyone*.

Of course, I blamed myself. If we hadn't been arguing, if I hadn't told the stubborn and beautiful boy enough was enough, that he needed to love me enough, love himself enough, to be honest about who he was and what we were, he would never have left that night wrapped in good-bye and silent acceptance that our relationship had run its course. I mean I logically knew he would have left regardless of the fight or not. His twin brother called needing a ride home and whenever one Archer brother needed something, the others were right there to offer it up. Especially the twins. Rule and Remy were two sides of the same tarnished coin and there would have been no stopping him, if Rule said he needed him. But . . . the giant but and uncertainty that haunted me to this day, if I hadn't said I'd had enough, if I hadn't told him I deserved someone that loved me fully and completely and openly the way I loved him, then maybe, just maybe, he would have been paying closer attention to the road. Maybe he would have seen the semi that lost control and could have avoided the collision. And, of course, the biggest maybe of all, maybe he would still be here with me.

I begged him to stay, to tell me that our love was enough to finally get him to come clean to his brothers, and asked him to set his best friend free from the shadows of half-truths and deception he had her trapped in, but all he could do was shake his head at me and look at me out of eyes the color of winter while he told me he couldn't do any of it. He wasn't ready, and he understood if that meant I had to move on to someone that was.

I wanted to hate him. To this day, all these years since the accident, I wanted to hate him, but I never could. My love for him was too big, too strong to leave room for any kind of hate, so instead I worked my ass off to heal people that were broken. Remy's body had broken the night of the crash, but there were things inside of him, fundamental issues that he should have addressed with not only himself but also his family well before we got to the serious stage of our relationship and definitely before we moved in together. Remy was broken on the inside and someone, namely me, should have tried to fix him before he was lost to me for good.

Thinking about broken men, I forced my attention back to the one in front of me as my assistant nudged up the speed on the treadmill Dominic was running on. We were going to see if he could last a full hour with the speed and incline increased every ten minutes. He had a mask on his face to measure his breathing, electrodes taped to his bare chest to monitor his heart rate, and various other contraptions clipped to him, so I had all the data I needed to see what kind of shape his body was in after the fall and all the surgeries to piece him back together.

We were at the halfway point and he was still keeping a pretty steady pace which I had to admit impressed the hell out of me. That shattered femur was no joke when it came to having a serious leg injury, but aside from a slight imbalance in his stride, he was weathering this first test well. He was sweaty, but his breathing seemed steady and his heart rate was better than some of the professional athletes I put through the same test.

Dominic Voss was built like an ancient Spartan. He looked like he had been crafted to be a warrior and protector since birth. Even with being laid up in the hospital while he healed he was still impossibly broad and toned. His shoulders looked like they could hold up the weight of the world and then some and I couldn't remember ever seeing an ass look that tight and perfect in a pair of track pants, which was saying a lot considering the bulk of my clientele got paid exorbitant amounts of money to look good in athletic gear.

I was taller than him by a few inches, but he was cut and hard in all the right places and that superb body and the intensity on the roughly hewn face attached to it were wreaking havoc on my concentration. I was supposed to be paying attention to how he responded to the tests, not to the way drops of sweat were running down the sides of his neck and across the impressive bulge of his pecs. And I really, really shouldn't be wondering what he would do if I leaned over the edge of the treadmill and licked the salty moisture away with my tongue.

I shifted my gaze away when my assistant caught me staring and nodded when he asked if he should kick up the speed some more. I nodded but watched Dom flinch a little as he had to adjust his gait to keep up with the machine. His dark eyebrows were furrowed. His already bronze complexion looked even darker and I could hear him breathing audibly behind the mask strapped to his face. I watched as his arms pumped hard at his sides, the left one flowing free and easily like it was supposed to while the right one moved stiffly and awkwardly. I didn't have any doubt that he could chase a bad guy down in a footrace, but I was starting to wonder if he could hold on to them when he caught up. His mobility on the left side was fluid and sure, the right side of his body looked like it should be attached to a much older man with arthritis.

He was struggling. But he wouldn't say anything. In fact, when the treadmill went up to the highest setting, which was the last ten minutes, he would run through and he didn't offer a single complaint. I frowned at him because I knew that that kind of exertion wasn't good for his leg. The body had its own language and if you refused to listen to what it was telling you, then chances were you were doing more harm than good. When my assistant asked to kick it up the last time, I shook my head in the negative and saw Dom's very dark green eyes narrow at me. I knew that if he didn't have the plastic ventilator covering the entire lower part of his face I would be getting an earful.

I met his look with a bland one of my own. I was in charge here and the sooner he learned that, the better this partnership would be. I kept my eyes locked on his and treated him to the same slow and thorough appraisal he had given me yesterday, only I got the added benefit of getting to check him out while he was sweaty and shirtless.

After Remy died, I went a little crazy. I figured if he couldn't love me enough to save us, to save himself, then I was obviously the problem. I figured I was nothing special, undeserving of someone as fantastic and charismatic as Remy Archer, so I went off the deep end. I slept around like it was a sport. I tried on boy after boy, searching for one that would fit. I burned through men like a wild fire endlessly searching for that special something that I'd had so briefly. I was trying to fuck away grief and guilt and there had been plenty of willing partners to help me do it.

Then one day I got a phone call out of the blue that changed everything. Remy's best friend, a sweet little thing named Shaw Landon, now Shaw Archer, wanted me to come and meet the other Archer boys. Remy's twin and his older brother were moving on in life, finding loves and lives of their own, but the way Remy went out . . . we all deserved more than secrets and speculation. She convinced me to come meet the entire family and like an insane person I agreed.

I had no clue how I could look Remy's twin in the eye and not fall to pieces. How could I look at the face of the only man I ever loved on another man and not fall apart? It turned out to be pretty easy.

As much as Rule and Remy looked alike, they were worlds and worlds apart. Where Remy had been polished and shined to perfection, Rule Archer was pierced and inked up in a beautiful riot of chaos. Remy's hair had been short and styled, Rule's was hot pink and spiked up like a weapon. They had the same face and the same eyes, but that was where all similarity stopped. Remy had been kind, loving, almost a pushover. Rule Archer was as in your face as any man I had ever met and he obviously didn't care if he impressed or offended.

Watching the family that loved the same man I did struggling to heal and doing it together through love and patience made me pull my head out of my ass. I stopped sleeping around, buckled down at school so I could get out and go to work, and put all my energy into helping others. I still dated here and there, but no one had that same effect on me that Remy Archer did. No one immediately touched my heart, and I was too busy and too focused on my career and making a difference in my clients' lives to notice the loss.

That's why my reaction to Dom was equally shocking and thrilling. When I first saw Remy and started to fall in love, it was like being surrounded by a fluffy blanket of good feelings and endless comfort. It was something I sunk into and never wanted to be without. It felt easy and as natural as breathing. The instant I laid eyes on the big, brooding cop, it was like a full body assault. There was nothing easy or comfortable about it. My ears started ringing like I had been knocked upside the head. My vision narrowed so that all I could see was him, and what I saw made my blood heat up and my heart thump loudly. My chest hurt and it was hard to breathe because all I could smell was the earthy, musky scent, that was far too alluring and oh so masculine, that emanated from him. My knees went slightly weak, which made me glad I was standing behind my desk, and it took me a solid three minutes before I could get my voice to work.

He was rougher-looking, more aggressive and assertive than the men I typically found attractive. He looked like he could easily take care of himself out on the streets and like he would have no trouble taking care of whoever he was in the bedroom with. Everything about him was dark and serious, from his short black hair to his intent olive-colored gaze that clearly showed his frustration and fear. His voice was deep and gravelly and the way it made my skin ripple in response had me needing to sit down and take a minute to pull myself together. I wasn't prepared for him. My reactions were completely visceral and primitive. All the responses Dominic Voss drew from me felt like they came from someplace elemental and animalistic. It was my reaction to him that scared the holy hell out of me.

As he pushed himself to complete the test, his muscles bulged and flexed. His broad chest expanded and contracted rapidly, making the white scars that crisscrossed his shoulder and side stand out in stark relief against the rest of his tawny skin. There was more evidence of his obviously risky line of work in the jagged scar that shot over his ear and along the side of his skull and contrasted with his short, dark hair. Everything about the man seemed dangerous and brutal, which wasn't something I should find appealing.

But I so did.

When the hour ended and the treadmill cranked down to a barely moving pace so he could cool down, he pulled the respiratory mask off and huffed out, "Not bad, right?"

He was still breathing heavily, but there was obvious pride hidden beneath his exertion.

I frowned a little bit and marked some things off on the chart I was using to track his vitals.

"How does your leg feel?"

He lifted a dark eyebrow at me and I watched as his hand went to his thigh. The corners of his mouth turned down in a scowl. "It's fine."

I made a noise in my throat and met his dark look with one of my own. I was stupidly attracted to the man, fascinated that after so long I had a genuine response to another man, but I had a job to do and his long term recovery was my priority, not getting him into bed.

"I think 'fine' is an exaggeration. I think you are pushing yourself too hard and your body is fighting back."

He continued to rub his thigh while lines of discomfort furrowed across his forehead. I took the opportunity to watch the enticing flex of muscle and sinew that was everywhere as he moved.

"Haven't you ever heard of playing through the pain? Yeah, it fucking hurts, everything fucking hurts, but I can't live my life waiting for it not to hurt before I start existing again."

I inhaled sharply and shifted my gaze back to the clipboard. I'd done my fair share of waiting for things to stop hurting before getting my life back on track and the reminder, even though he didn't know anything about me, stung, and the fear of living and losing what mattered most nipped at all of my senses.

"If you work the muscles so hard that they never get the chance to fully repair themselves, you'll never get your natural stride back. If you push yourself too hard, you'll never recover from your injuries, and where you are now is the best that you'll ever be."

He grunted and stepped off the treadmill. "Then tell me what to do and I'll do it."

I had to bite my tongue—hard—from spitting out the really inappropriate things I wanted to ask him to do.

Things like step closer.

Things like let me touch him all over.

Things like let me kiss everything that hurts so I could make it better.

I closed my hand around the pen I was using to make notes so tightly the plastic casing snapped.

My assistant and my new patient both looked at me

curiously as I cleared my throat and awkwardly took a step away from the heat I could feel coming off of Dom's half-naked body.

"I can give you the tools to make your body work better, but you have to listen to what it's telling you. I'm not saying that you shouldn't push past the pain in order to get results, but you need to be able to tell the difference between something simply hurting and something being irrevocably damaged."

That was what condition I thought my heart was going to be in after I lost Remy, but now the twinges it was having, the twitches it was displaying at the nearness of this man, made me wonder if it, like Dom, had been injured and pushed too hard to heal before it was ready.

Dom's dark head bent down so that he was looking at the tips of his tennis shoes. He put his hands on his lean hips and I saw his wide shoulders hunch forward. He looked like he was suddenly being weighed down with the truth of how serious his situation was and that his natural-born fight may have been doing more harm than good.

"I just want to get back to how I was."

I reached out a hand before I could stop myself and put it on his shoulder. His skin was warm, vital and throbbing with so much life under my fingertips. His head jerked up at the contact and our eyes locked. It felt like the most meaningful conversation I had ever had was happening even though no words were exchanged as we looked at each other.

"There is no going back but there is accepting your

new normal." That was one of the hardest lessons I had had to learn along the way.

Those massive shoulders went back, his army-green eyes gleamed at me, and I almost passed out when the full impact of the sexy grin he unleashed hit me.

"I'll accept that there might not be any going back, but there is going forward and from where I'm standing what's in front of me is anything but normal."

He might be a bruiser and far more blunt in his manner and with his words than I was used to, but as we continued to watch each other I had to admit it was a nice change of pace to see the intensity of the things I was feeling reflected right back at me.

There was nothing subtle or hidden about Dominic Voss and that forthrightness was irresistible and a balm to the hidden parts of me that were just as broken as his body was.

Chapter Three

Dominic

I HURT ALL over.

It was a different hurt than the searing and relentless pain that had taken up residence in my shoulder and leg since the accident, this was more of a constant ache, a heavy throb that lived deep in all of my muscles and reminded me every waking moment that there was still work to do. I always considered myself to be in excellent shape and worked hard to make sure that I could not only keep up with the bad guys but with all the other guys on the force. After spending a week getting my ass handed to me by Lando I understood that just being able to bench-press my own weight didn't mean shit about being fit.

He had me doing all kinds of things to build my strength back up and all kinds of things I had never done before to stretch the injured parts of my body out and build in new flexibility and elasticity I hadn't even known I needed. I did everything he told me to do even when it felt like my joints were going to pop out of the sockets and even when it felt like my lungs were going to catch on fire and burn up. I couldn't remember ever working as hard for anything in my life but the dull ache in my shoulder as I reached for the beer in front of me without a struggle or any kind of awkwardness reminded me that hard work and a little pain was indeed leading to results.

I still had a slight limp but it wasn't as noticeable and the mobility that I had gained back in my shoulder was mind-blowing considering the short amount of time I had spent with the sexy trainer. He pushed me hard and I in turn grumbled at him about it and flirted with him shamelessly, in part to keep my mind off of how hard the paces he was putting me through were, but mostly because he was gorgeous and I found the way he ran hot and cold with me fascinating.

He watched me the same way I watched him and occasionally when I tossed out an offhanded quip about our obvious attraction, he would look like he was considering taking our relationship to a different level but he always shut it down and kept things coolly professional.

"So why don't you just ask him out?" Royal was sitting across from me at the bar I had asked her to meet me at for a drink after a particularly grueling round of therapy. She'd just gotten off of patrol and I could tell by the tight pull of her mouth and the shadows in her chocolate-colored eyes that it hadn't been a great shift. I wanted to ask her what happened, but I honestly wasn't sure I could handle the jealousy that would claw at me when she talked about doing the only thing I wanted to do.

Royal was the best friend a guy could ever ask for and she knew me better than anyone, aside from my family. I didn't have to go into details about the heady sexual tension that was pulsing between me and the handsome physical therapist, she could tell by all the things I wasn't saying and by the frown that I couldn't seem to shake.

"Because I need his help more than I need to get laid, and I don't want to offend him or make him uncomfortable if he's flat-out not interested." Even if he gave off very interested vibes when he thought I wasn't paying attention.

She made a face and pushed some of her long, auburn hair over her shoulder. What can I say? Redheads were my favorite, and she was the prettiest girl I had ever seen. I felt like I had been keeping her safe from not only overzealous boys but also from herself since the first moment we met. She always deserved more than to be just another pretty face and she worked hard to prove it. We were kindred that way. No one had ever questioned my ability to do my job, but I never wanted to give them the chance to.

"Well then, once you're all back to one hundred percent and back on the force, then you can ask him out and the worst that can happen is he can say no."

I grunted a response, because being rejected by Lando on a personal level really did seem like the worst thing that could happen, which was insane considering the reason I had him in my life in the first place.

"I need to worry about getting my job back, not getting a date." I lifted an eyebrow at her as she smiled a little sadly at me. "I miss it. I miss you. How's the new partner working out?"

She sat back in the seat across from me and fiddled with the label on her drink. Her dark brown eyes shifted to the tabletop and I saw her bite on her lip. I blinked a little and scolded myself for asking something I didn't really want to know the answer to in the first place. Life went on whether I wanted it to or not, and I could tell by her almost guilty expression that Royal was enjoying being on patrol with a cop that was not me.

"It's good. He's good. It's different working with someone that hasn't known me since I was five, but I miss you, too, Dom, and I want you back at work as soon as possible."

I copied her pose and lifted a hand to rub it over the top of my short hair in frustration. "You want me back, but you don't want to be my partner anymore, do you?"

She flushed and tapped her fingers nervously on the side of her beer bottle. Royal was my best friend in the entire world and I would do anything for her, even if it meant letting her go.

"When you fell off that building and I thought I was watching you die right in front of me, it was the worst thing that had ever happened to me. I couldn't be a cop in that moment because I was so worried about you and I couldn't be a good cop after, because I was convinced it was my fault you got hurt. I don't think about the new guy that way. He's my partner, I have his back, we're a team, but I don't feel like my life is going to be over if something bad happens to him. Does that make sense?"

I grunted again and finished the rest of my beer. It wasn't what I wanted to hear, but it made sense. "There are no guarantees I'm going to be deemed fit enough for duty anyway. I want you to be the best cop you can be even if it's partnered with someone that isn't me. I've always wanted what is best for you, Royal."

She bit down on her lip even harder and lowered her head, but not before I saw a sheen of tears flash over the surface of her dark eyes. "You *will* be back, Dom. I know you will."

It was depressing to think about any other option, so I changed the subject with all the subtlety of a bulldozer. "How are things going with your southern charmer?"

I wasn't the biggest fan of Royal's new boyfriend and it wasn't just because the guy had a criminal record and a smile that could charm the pants off of even the most jaded of hearts. I couldn't trust a guy who was that pretty and that smooth. I honestly believed he cared about Royal, but he had already broken her heart once and that was pretty much impossible to come back from in my book. I tried to play nice because I knew she was gone for the guy and he was it for her, but generally I just stayed away and stayed out of their relationship. I knew Royal was hoping I warmed up to Asa eventually, but I didn't see it happening anytime soon.

A smile made her already stunning face truly beautiful in the way only love could. "Things are good. I wasn't sure how moving in together so quickly was going to work out, but so far so good." She laughed a little. "Plus he always comes to get me when I lock myself out of places and never complains. That automatically makes him a keeper in my book."

She was happy. Really, truly happy and more than that she was settling into the person she had always struggled to be. There was no more doubt about the choices she had made and the path she was on. Royal was owning the things that had always made her so special and unique and I couldn't be happier for her.

I was about to tell her as much when a familiar tall figure suddenly cut through the crowd at the bar. I shouldn't have been surprised to see him here considering the bar I picked was close to the gym, so I didn't have to go far after my therapy session, but it was still startling to see him outside of the serious and professional setting I was used to spending time with him in. I let my eyes roll over him as he caught sight of me and faltered a little. Instead of being dressed in his typical polo shirt and pressed slacks, he had on a pair of track pants similar to mine and a white tank top. His rust-colored hair was tousled on the top of his head and if I had to wager a guess, I would bet he had just come from doing a workout of his own.

I watched the indecision flash across his pale eyes before he veered off and made his way over to where I was sitting. He stopped by the edge of the table and dipped his chin down in a slight nod. I couldn't keep my gaze off of the smattering of freckles that dotted the tops of his strong-looking shoulders and that danced along the curve of his toned biceps.

"Hey."

I motioned to Royal, who was looking between the two of us in an almost comical fashion, and introduced them. "Orlando Frederick, this is my best friend, Royal Hastings. She also used to be my partner on the force."

She stuck out a hand and gave the other man a cheesy grin as he shook it. I wanted to kick her but figured that would be too obvious.

"I'm so happy you agreed to help him. We can't wait to put him back to work." She looked at me and blinked too-wide eyes in an overtly obvious manner. "It was so nice to meet you, but I have to run. I'm supposed to meet my man for dinner." She slipped off the stool and winked at me. "And dessert. Keep up the good work and I'll be in touch."

Before I could stop her, she was gone and Lando had slipped into her empty seat. A waitress came by and he ordered a vodka and tonic and another beer for me.

"She's adorable." It was pretty safe as far as small talk went and Royal was one of my favorite subjects.

"She is and she knows it. She's actually the one that got me the referral to get in and meet with you. Her boyfriend works with someone that pulled the strings."

He crossed his arms and leaned forward a little bit on the table and I told myself not to drool or say anything stupid as I watched his muscles tense and flex with the motion.

"Rome Archer." His eyebrows pulled down slightly and his denim-colored eyes flashed with something that looked very lost and sad. "There isn't much I wouldn't do for the Archers."

I didn't know most of the people that Royal had been spending time with since my injury and since getting involved with Asa, but I did know they seemed like a good group of people and they took care of my girl for me when I wasn't able to.

I shrugged. "I don't know him, but I'm grateful he put in a good word for me."

Lando nodded and we lapsed into an awkward silence while we waited for the drinks to arrive. When the waitress put the rocks glass down in front of him, he ran a finger around the rim of it and looked at me from under his eyelashes.

"I'm not really much of a drinker, but it's been a long week." I didn't know him well, but I could distinctly hear a hint of accusation in his tone.

I picked up my beer and narrowed my eyes at him. "Why is that?" I was the one with the sore muscles and burning tendons. I should be the one drinking for the strength to keep going, not him.

He picked his drink up and finished it all in one, healthy swallow. He set the rocks glass down and stood up to dig his wallet out of his pocket. He tossed some money on the table and took a few steps so that he was standing at my elbow. I looked up at him as he bent his head down just enough that he could speak directly into my ear. A full body shiver worked its way across my skin as his voice rasped, "You are distractingly good-looking, Dominic, but I don't date my clients, and I don't think I could ever get involved with a cop."

I was too stunned to react for a moment and in those

few seconds he managed to push away from the table and make his way towards the door. By the time I managed to fumble my own wallet out of my back pocket and pay for my own drinks, he was out the door, but I was used to chasing down my prey even if I wasn't as fast as I used to be. I caught up to him in the parking lot of the clinic as he was approaching a sleek-looking sports car.

I put a hand on his shoulder and was already tearing into him before he turned fully around to face me.

"I don't know what I find more insulting, the fact that you just assume I want to date you or the fact that I'm a cop somehow makes me beneath you. You have a lot of nerve, Mr. Fancy-Pants, a lot of nerve and a lot of ego."

I was pissed and offended. I was also hurt and a little bit embarrassed. I didn't like anything about all of it. Sure the guy was ridiculously attractive and I had never been drawn to anyone the way I was instantly drawn to him, but that didn't mean I was asking him to move in together and get married. A little harmless flirting and some innocent eye fucking shouldn't have landed me in the shame corner and I wanted him to know it. I was opening my mouth to finish giving him a piece of my mind when I was cut off by hard hands on either of my shoulders pushing me backwards into the side of the car behind me.

I grunted at the contact and at the surprise of chilly metal against my back while my front was suddenly pressed all along a rigid and hard male body.

He might look distinguished and fancy, but he kissed rough and dirty. His hands were hard on my shoulders as he leaned into me and held me in place while his mouth moved over mine. I put a hand on the lean curve of his waist and met him move for move because I'd kissed plenty of boys in my time but never one that made my head spin to the point that it made me forget where I was.

His lips were soft, but there was hard passion behind them. He kissed me like he was angry that he wanted to kiss me, but I wasn't going to complain about being handled like that. I liked the abrasion, liked the almost desperate way he held on to me, and I liked that he felt as solid and heavy as I did as we continued to press closer and closer together. I offered zero resistance when the tip of his tongue brushed across the seam of my lips. I let him in, in fact, I couldn't wait to let him in and get him closer. I tugged on his waist until we were hip to hip and I felt him take in the heated gasp that escaped when I felt his arousal press against my own.

His skin was soft, almost baby smooth as our faces touched, and I found the contrast between that softness and the hardness of the rest of him alluring and exciting. His muscles were tense and hard, but they felt like they were encased in velvet and silk. I wanted to know if the rest of him felt the same way.

One of his hands slid around the back of my skull and he pulled me even closer still as he continued to devour my mouth like it was the only opportunity he was ever going to have to act on his baser impulses. I was getting ready to put a hand under the hem of his tank that had ridden up just a little over a set of abs that I wanted to touch and was slightly envious of when a loud beep from one of the cars next to us startled us apart.

We were both breathing heavy and watching each other with wary eyes as we put some space between one another. Lando blew out a deep breath and shoved both of his hands through his already messy hair. His pale eyes were serious as he told me, "You won't be my client forever, Dom, but you will be a cop for the foreseeable future. I already lost someone I cared about and I barely came back from the pain of that. I'm not a strong enough man to care about someone that purposely puts themselves at risk . . . even if you are more than tempting."

I leaned back against the car he had just ravaged me against and watched him silently while he slipped behind the wheel of his sports car and pulled out of the spot.

Huh . . . that was interesting, to say the least, and even though we had only known each other for a week, he had to know I was the kind of guy that thrived on a challenge and on overcoming obstacles. Besides, our entire relationship was based on healing and it was starting to look like I wasn't the only one with wounds that needed some attention.

Chapter Four

Lando

I WAS HOPING the rhythmic pounding of my feet on the treadmill and the sound of weights clanking together would be enough to drown out the endless lecture about common sense and impulse control I had been giving myself since I lost my damn mind and kissed Dom. The "what were you thinking" was colliding against the "when can we do that again and again and again" in a symphony of noise and emotion that was so loud and overwhelming I just wanted to hide from it all.

I'd always been allowed to love openly and physically within my family and group of friends. There wasn't so much as a batted eye the first time I brought a boyfriend home, and it wasn't long into my relationship with Remy that my mom had started dropping hints about marriage and kids even though neither one of us was old enough to consider either of those things at the time. I'd never been shy about expressing my interest or availability to someone that I was attracted to, but I'd also never been compelled to attack a man with my mouth before either.

When I met Remy, it was love at first sight. I had started seeing forever and a life together before we even shared our first kiss. With Dom, I couldn't see anything but those sharp army-green eyes and my own rampaging lust shining back at me. Instant attraction could be fun and a nice boost to the ego, but whatever was happening between the two of us felt bigger than that. It felt big enough to rival the fear that always lingered just under the surface whenever I started to develop feelings for someone. It felt like it had a life of its own and couldn't be controlled by either my rules or my sense of self-preservation and that terrified me. Not to mention the fact I had mauled the guy knowing good and well that I was going to have to see him as soon as the weekend was over. I was both horrified and frustrated that it was a kiss I was going to have to ignore . . . even though it was the best kiss I could remember having in a really, really long time.

Annoyed at the kick in my gut as I replayed that kiss over and over again, I glanced to my side at the woman running on the treadmill next to me. I didn't immediately recognize her, which meant she must be pretty new to the gym and she seemed to be thinking just as hard as she scowled and muttered under her breath while she ran.

She was tall and had a perfectly sleek blond ponytail

that bobbed on the top of her head as she moved. Everything she was wearing was monochromatic and pretty boring considering she had a body that was designed to make straight men do really stupid things. She was stunning and if I liked girls, she would probably be the type that caught my eye. Hell, I didn't like girls like that and she still caught my attention. I must have been staring because she turned her head and stormy blue eyes locked on mine. I lifted an eyebrow at her because even though she was running at a nice clip she wasn't breathing hard or dripping with sweat. I was impressed.

She stumbled a little when our eyes locked and blushed charmingly as I grinned at her. I hit the controls on the treadmill to slow the belt down to a light jog.

"Are you a new member?" The gym was below the clinic and while I typically used the equipment upstairs, I thought the other people and noise would distract me from my wayward thoughts and rebelling libido.

She slowed her machine down as well and lifted a shoulder in a shrug. "Not really. I usually come in before work during the week or try to catch a yoga class after a full day in court." She shrugged again. "I'm a lawyer. I can use all the stress relief I can get, plus I haven't been sleeping well, so . . ." She trailed off and blushed again like she was surprised she had said so much to a total stranger.

"Ahhh . . . I'm usually with clients in the morning and I only do yoga with them if I think it will help with their therapy regimen. I actually own the gym and the rehabilitation clinic with a few business partners. Orlando

Frederick." I stuck out my hand but had to wait until she shut the machine all the way off before she would take it.

"I'm a klutz. I would take us both down if I tried to shake while moving. Sayer Cole."

I grinned at her when she told me her name. "A very pretty name for a very pretty lady."

She blinked at me like she didn't understand the words I was using and then tilted her head to the side and looked at me consideringly. "Yours is kind of unusual. I'm not sure if it's the red hair or not, but you really don't look like an Orlando."

I turned my machine off as well and let her get away with changing the subject in her very lawyerly way. "I know. I think my folks should have gone with Harry so I could cash in on the whole royal ginger thing, but no. My dad was a recruiter for a few different sports teams when I was younger, so we moved around a lot. All of us kids have names of cities. Mom won't confirm or deny that's where we were conceived, but I have a brother named Austin and a sister named Phoenix. Most people just call me Lando."

I waited a second to see if she would elaborate on her own interesting moniker but when she just continued to watch me without saying anything we lapsed into an awkward silence. I was going to tell her it was nice to meet her and tell her I hoped she enjoyed the facilities when she suddenly shook her head and gave me a rueful grin.

"It doesn't matter how fast or how long I run, I can't seem to get away from the things chasing me, but it was nice to have a little company while I tried."

I crossed my arms on the safety bar and leaned towards her. "I'm kind of in the same boat." I arched both my eyebrows up. "Boy trouble?"

I couldn't explain why I was pressing her, but there was something about her that tugged at me. She seemed very put together, almost polished and practiced in a way that made her seem untouchable, but there was a hint of vulnerability in her bright blue eyes that was begging for any kind of basic human connection.

She shook her head slowly and reached for a bottle of water that was by her feet. "Not a boy at all. A man. A man that is all kinds of the wrong kind of man, but that doesn't matter because I still have a crush on him." She made a face. "A crush. I've never had a crush on anyone in my entire life and I have no idea what to do with it, or with him."

She sounded baffled and adorable. I just wanted to hug her and ask her if she needed a friend. I ran my hands over my damp hair because I wasn't blessed with ice water in my veins like my new companion and did sweat when I ran.

"In my experience as long as he treats you right and appreciates you then no man is the wrong kind of man." I winced as my own advice kicked me in the balls.

A man that put himself in danger and risked his life because he was a protector, a hero, well, that wasn't exactly the wrong kind of man, but it was wrong for me because I was unable to get my head around caring about someone and losing them again. My heart just wasn't up for it even if the rest of me was all on board.

She must have seen the battle waging inside of me on my face because she reached out a hand and put it on my shoulder and squeezed. She didn't come off as the touchy-feely type, so my distress must have been pretty evident to the pretty stranger.

"You're right. He's not the wrong kind of man at all, but that doesn't keep me from being the wrong kind of woman." She let her hand fall and took a step back. "It was really lovely to meet you, Lando. I hope I get to see you around again." It was her turn to lift her eyebrows up at me. "And I hope you figure out your boy trouble, because the chances I'll figure out mine are slim to none."

She walked away and I was going to head over to the free weights and see if the clanking of metal on metal could get my head out of Dom's pants and off his lips when my phone rang from the pocket of my track pants. I knew it was my mom by the ringtone and if I let it go to voice mail, she would more than likely show up at the gym to check on me. I was close to my entire family, so it wasn't often that I didn't check in or keep them updated on what was happening in my life. Ever since Dominic Voss walked into my office just a few short days ago, I hadn't been doing anything I normally did.

I touched the screen and put the phone to my ear and changed directions so I could head up to my office and talk to her without the noise in the background.

"Hey, Ma. What's up?"

"Your father and I got a new financial advisor to handle our retirement since your dad is set on buying an

RV and touring the world. He's handsome and single. I gave him your number."

I sighed and flopped down in my chair. I loved my mom, but she was desperate for me to finally settle down and be happy. She had a habit of handing my phone number out to any male she encountered that had a good job, was reasonably attractive, and single. She didn't bother vetting if they were gay or not, which had led to more than one awkward conversation my father had to smooth over on her behalf.

"Ma." I rubbed a hand over my face and blurted out, "I met someone." I immediately wanted to take it back as she squealed into my ear, but I had always been open and honest with her and it was like the truth was just looking for an excuse to escape from somewhere deep down inside of me.

She was jabbering so fast and at such a high-pitched octave I could barely understand her. "What's his name? What's he look like? What's he do for a living? Is he close with his family? How long have you been seeing him?"

I let the rapid-fire questions bombard me until she wore herself out. I sighed and told her, "He's a client, Ma, and a cop."

She went really quiet on the other end of the phone and then whispered so softly that I almost didn't hear her, "Oh, Lando . . ."

I rubbed my temples and grunted. "I know, Ma. Believe me, I know. The reason he came to see me is because he was already hurt in the line of duty. He got shot and fell off of a building." Just saying the words made me tense up. Dom was so lucky to be alive, and I couldn't fathom how hard he was working to put himself back in the line of fire after a close call like that.

She was quiet for another drawn out minute before solemnly asking me, "Are you sure you can handle being with someone in such a high-risk field? After Remy . . ." she trailed off again and I had to fight the urge to bang my forehead on the edge of my desk.

"I know how I was after Remy, Ma. I'm still that way minus the sleeping around. I think I'll always be that way. I don't think being with this guy is an option for me. First of all, he's a client, so anything romantic between us is pretty goddamn unprofessional, and I honestly don't think I'm strong enough to get involved with someone that I could very well lose."

She made a little noise and I could almost see her lifting her hand to her mouth. She cleared her throat and when she spoke, she sounded like the woman that had always told me to be proud of who I was and to chase after whatever dream I had. "You've never been afraid of anything in your life, Orlando. Fear was the biggest issue in your relationship with Remy. It controlled everything that sweet boy did and we all hated to watch him live like that. It broke your heart time and time again. We taught you better than to let fear rule you and maybe I forgot that because you scared me when Remy died. I let my fear take over. You lost so much of yourself when you lost that boy, and maybe I've been scared to see you go back there, but that's not who you are and that's not who we are. You've never been afraid to love anyone. Don't start now."

I gave her a dry little chuckle and leaned back in the chair so that I could stare up at the ceiling. "A little early to be talking about love, Ma."

But I did like him. I liked that he was effortlessly charismatic and brash. I liked that he was determined and driven in the way only someone with real dedication could be. I liked that he didn't bother to hide his attraction to me but kept in check and in control because I obviously couldn't be trusted to. I liked that he could give just as good as he got and that he felt hot and hard when he was pressed against me. And I liked that I liked him. It had been way too long since I found anyone interesting enough to engage with and I liked the pop and sizzle of desire that worked under my skin and made my blood heat when I was around him. That was new.

Of course, I'd wanted Remy and a few of the men that had come after, but none of them blindsided me with lust. No one made me feel like I was being buried under my own hunger and scrambling to fight my way through thick and slippery passion. I couldn't get my footing or find anything to hold on to, which meant I was falling. I didn't like the feeling one bit.

"You haven't mentioned a man in a long time, kiddo. Regardless if this one is a client or not, that means something. I think you owe it to yourself to figure out what that something is, don't you?"

"Maybe. I gotta go. Tell Dad that if he gets an RV I get to borrow it to go camping."

She laughed. "Will do. Figure out what you're gonna do about the cop and then bring him for dinner. I get tired of harassing your sister and brother about my future grandchildren."

I rolled my eyes and told her I would call her later.

I had no clue what I was going to do about the hot cop, but I needed to figure it out fast because I didn't want to make a fool of myself when he showed up for his therapy session on Monday. I'd already mauled him with my mouth, if I didn't get a handle on my reaction to him there was a very good chance I could be inspired to attack him with the rest of my body as well. Something told me Dom wouldn't complain about being ravaged, but my mom was right. There was something more there, something that hadn't been there for a very long time and I owed it to myself and to Dominic to be man enough to face it and find out what that something was, if only I could reach around the walls of fear to get at it.

Chapter Five

Dominic

LANDO WAS ANGRY at me and doing a piss-poor job of hiding it. Not that I could blame him.

I had apparently undone all the positive improvement he had put into my body over the previous week by not knowing when enough was enough. I wanted to pretend like I was still the guy that could do everything, could still be the one everyone counted on when they needed a strong back and some good old-fashioned sweat, but I wasn't. After helping my youngest sister, Ari, move into her very first apartment on Saturday I should have told Royal no when she asked if I wanted to go hiking with her on Sunday. As a result of the overuse, my thigh felt like it was made of Jell-O and I was pretty sure that there was a torn muscle or strained tendon somewhere in my shoulder. I was back to hurting like everything inside of me was on fire and even the simplest of movements made me wince.

Lando was watching me with a furious scowl on his handsome face. I wanted to tell him the fierce expression was ruined by his freckles, but I didn't think he was in the mood to flirt. He looked like he wanted to knock me around and yell at me.

"Come on. It was my little sister. I couldn't exactly tell her no when she asked for my help. I practically raised her when my dad died when we were younger. I've always been her go-to guy. I didn't think it would hurt anything."

His pale eyes narrowed just a fraction at me. "You were wrong. There isn't any point in trying to put you through your set routine today. You can't even lift that twenty-pound dumbbell up past your waist."

I went to heft the weight up to show him that he was wrong and ended up yelping in pain and dropping the heavy metal back on the floor with a loud thud. He had to jump back a step to avoid getting his toes crushed as I let out a litany of swear words and reached up to cradle my screaming shoulder. I swore again as he gave me an "I told you so" look and bent to pick up the weight I couldn't lift like it was a feather. He walked over to put it on the rack and came back with his arms crossed over his chest.

I thought there might be a level of awkwardness between us after his kiss-and-run, but he was so overly irritated that I had overworked myself that there didn't seem to be much room for anything else to work between us at the moment.

"Hey, I'm sorry, okay. This whole being half of what

I used to be is taking some getting used to, and I really never have told Ari no before."

He sighed and released his arms so that he could shove his hands through his hair. I watched the way the motion lifted the edge of his shirt up over the top of his black pants. He even had a dusting of freckles that zigzagged below his belly button. I wanted to see how far down they went. I wanted to know so badly it made my mouth water and my fingers curl into my palms with the effort it took to keep my hands to myself.

"I'm upset that you are hurting. I get that you're frustrated, that you would love to see immediate results and get back to work, but that isn't how these kinds of injuries work. I don't like to see anyone in pain when it can be avoided." He let his arms fall and caught me looking at him with what I'm sure was a fairly predatory gleam in my eye. I wanted it to be my turn to pounce. "Since you can't do any work with the weights, let's take a different route today. How about an hour of hot yoga and then a deep tissue massage?"

I grunted and climbed to my feet so that we were standing face to face and almost touching. "Can I say yes to one and no to the other?" I'd never done yoga a day in my life, and what the hell was hot yoga? It sounded dumb and uncomfortable. I couldn't see any logical reason to sweat my ass off.

"No." His tone was flat and the expression on his face left little room for argument. "If you want to stay with the program, then don't hurt yourself on your off days. We have to work around your stubbornness." The corner of his mouth kicked up in a grin that made me suck in a sharp breath. "And don't think you're too tough for yoga. It's taken down bigger and badder men than you, Officer Voss."

I rolled my shoulder and winced as lightning bolts of pain shot down my entire back. "All right. Let's get it over with, so we can move on to the massage part. Are you the one handling that as well?" *Please say yes, please say yes.* The chat rattled around inside my head along with images of him standing over me with oil-slick hands as he rubbed out all the knots and kinks in my injured shoulder. I could so work with that.

He didn't answer my question as he motioned for me to follow him out of the main area we had been using for the physical therapy session and took me past his office and down a set of stairs that emptied into a big, empty room that was obviously used for classes and group activities. He shut the door, fiddled with the controls on the wall which made the room immediately jump up in temperature, and suddenly I felt like I was walking through a muggy swamp and not standing in a gym. I tugged at the collar of my shirt as Lando walked over and pulled the shades on the massive windows that looked out into the rest of the gym down below. He smirked at me as he effectively cocooned us in the room that was rapidly heating up. He handed me a couple of mats that felt like they were made of rubber and told me to lay them out on the floor a few feet apart from one another.

"Since I want you to actually give this an honest shot

we'll keep it private, so it's just you and me. Give me ten minutes to go change into gym clothes."

I scowled a little and tugged at the fabric of my T-shirt that was already starting to stick to my chest. "I'm going to melt if you take any longer than that."

"Good. Maybe if I make you uncomfortable enough, you'll remember to take it easy on yourself. I'll be right back."

He went back up the set of stairs that had led us into the room and since there was only a narrow bench along one wall to sit on, I flopped down on the mat on the floor and stared up at the ceiling. Getting up from this position with my bum leg was going to be a bitch. I scowled at the thought and only lasted another minute before I had to peel my shirt off.

It was hotter than hell in the room and every second that passed, it felt like it was getting hotter. If I wasn't worried that it would send Lando running and totally cross the boundaries between personal and professional, I would've stripped my lightweight sweats off as well and done the damn yoga in my underwear. It would be way more interesting that way.

I was chuckling to myself at the thought when I heard him making his way back across the room. I lifted my head up from the floor to watch his approach and almost swallowed my tongue. He wasn't in his underwear, but he might as well have been. All he was wearing was a pair of loose, black basketball shorts and lots of naked skin. Pretty, pale, freckled skin. I liked it. I liked him and I wanted to touch him. The long and lean lines of muscles that flexed as he made his way over to me and took a seat on the mat next to mine were mesmerizing. I was in good shape, cut and defined better than most of the guys I worked with on the force, but this guy was perfect. He looked like the sculptures the ancients used to carve out of marble when they were depicting what the perfect male form should be. It was distracting to say the least, and I missed that he was talking to me because I was gawking at him like a love-struck teenager.

I cleared my throat and pushed myself up into a seated position. "I didn't hear a word you just said. If you want me to pay attention to you, then I'm telling you right now you need to put a shirt on." I was dead serious.

It was his turn to let his eyes rove over my torso and I didn't miss the way the blue burned through the gray the longer he looked at me. That look made me sweat twice as much as the heat swirling around the room.

He muttered something under his breath and climbed to his feet. "Okay so just follow what I do and try and concentrate on breathing. Don't work against your body, work with it. I don't think I can give you the entire spiel again either."

I went to push myself up from the ground and almost collapsed back when my shoulder hollered in protest. Lando immediately reached out a hand to help me up and it was there again when our palms touched, that spark, that flash of intensity that made every nerve ending I had stand to attention and beg to be pressed up against his slick skin.

I hissed out a breath between my teeth and watched as he shook his head a little, like he needed to clear it.

"Okay, so first bend over and put your hands flat on the floor like this." I watched him bend over with his legs perfectly straight as he put his hands flat in front of his feet. I tried to mimic the pose but barely got halfway there before I had to bend my knees.

He turned his head to the side and looked at me while he was upside down. "Your flexibility could use some work."

I grunted at him and tried to straighten up. "Thanks for noticing."

He chuckled and moved into some pose that looked like he was firing an invisible bow and arrow at the capital. I followed suit and was surprised that the pull in my shoulder ached but didn't bellow in pain. I was also surprised when Lando asked me quietly, "How many sisters do you have?"

It was the first thing he had ever asked that didn't have to do with my injury or regular routine. "Uh, two. Ari is a freshman in college and Greer just graduated. She wants to be a teacher."

He shifted poses again, this time lifting his hands up above his head like he was praying and pulling them down slowly while he balanced on one leg. I decided that if I was going to balance on one leg it wouldn't be the one I shattered and was pleased as hell that I didn't topple over.

"I have a little sister that's a senior in high school and a total nightmare for my parents. My dad can't keep the boys away. My little brother is a year younger than me and lives overseas so he can play professional soccer."

"Are you close with your family?" I was breathing harder than I expected to and I could hardly see through the rivers of sweat running down my face. It was a different kind of workout then I was used to, but my muscles were definitely straining and pulling. He dropped into what looked like a stationary push-up and I went to follow but paused. "I don't know if my shoulder is up to this."

"You have to bend your elbows and balance your weight. It's all about finding your center and letting your whole body bear the weight, not just the large muscle groups." I stretched my legs out behind me and went to push up but stopped before I got off the floor when his hands were on the center of my back and curving over my biceps to get me in the correct position. It felt like flames were dancing along every part of my bare skin where he touched me. "I'm super tight with my family. They've always been very supportive of me. How about you?"

When I levered up and balanced on my toes I waited with bated breath for my leg to give out or for my shoulder to flat-out collapse under the strain, but with my elbows bent and his hands holding me where I was supposed to be, I kept myself perfectly horizontal to the floor with minimal effort. I blew out a long breath and told him, "My family is just the girls and my mom. My dad was killed on duty when I was ten. My mom never remarried or got serious with anyone until us kids were older, so all we had was each other." I wheezed a little as my arms finally started to shake so I let him push me back to the ground and followed the guide of his hands as he had me bow my torso back so that I was arched up looking at him upside down as he stood over me.

"You father was a police officer as well?"

"Yeah."

"And even though you lost him you wanted to follow in his steps?" He sounded puzzled by my career choice and he wasn't the only one. My mother cried for a week straight when I was accepted into the academy. Even though all I had ever wanted to do was follow in my dad's footsteps.

"Being a cop was the only option for me. I never considered anything else. That's part of the reason why I'm so anxious to get back to it. I don't have a backup plan, Lando. This is it for me." It came sounding a little more raw and desperate than I intended it to, but it was the truth. I didn't know what I was going to do with myself if I couldn't go back on patrol and that was terrifying.

"Hmm . . ." He switched things around so that I was sitting upright and had a leg bent in front of me and my entire torso wrapped around it like a pretzel. I narrowed my eyes at him because he made it look effortless and I was actually breathing heavily and sweating buckets and not just from the temperature in the room. "Why was that it for you? You lost your father; you had to see how it hurt your mother and sisters and I bet they worry about you all the time. Why would you pick that as your only option?"

It was a good question. One I wasn't sure I had an answer to. "I wanted to make my dad proud. I wanted to help people. I wanted a job where no one would question my authority or my . . ." I yelped as I bent too far and my thigh protested. I rolled over and ended up on my back as I looked up at him. He was shiny with sweat from the heat in the room and his eyes were intently focused on me.

"Your masculinity or your sexuality? You wanted a job that was associated with being a man even if you just happened to be attracted to other men?"

I crossed my hands and rested them on my abs as my breath whooshed in and out. "Maybe that was part of it as I got older, but as far back as I can remember I wanted to wear a uniform and to carry a badge. I wanted to make a difference." I closed my eyes and drifted back in time. "I wanted to make sure no one else had to stand by their father's grave holding their mother's hand while she sobbed and sobbed."

"She very easily could be standing next to your grave next, Dominic." The words were so quiet it was almost like he breathed them instead of spoke them and there wasn't anything I could say to argue that he was wrong because he wasn't.

"I know, but I'm a cop. It's part of who I am and my mom has always accepted me for every single part of me. It sounds like we're both lucky that way."

He put his hands on his hips and seemed to be turning my words over in his head. After a couple of minutes where I just laid there and sweated, he finally spoke. "Why don't you take five and then meet me back upstairs in the spa area. We'll get the massage out of the way and see if we can work that shoulder out so that on Wednesday we can get back on track."

I struggled back into a seated position and lifted an eyebrow at him. "You never answered me. Are you the one handling the massage?"

His eyes flared hot at the center and the corners of his mouth twitched like he wanted to grin but was fighting the urge. "I shouldn't, we have techs, but I'm going to." The look on his face turned entirely predatory. "I have a feeling my self-control is going to be hurting as badly as your shoulder is by the time we're done."

I groaned as I watched him walk away. Basketball shorts did wonders for him both coming and going. "No pain no gain, Mr. Fancy-Pants."

Chapter Six

Lando

I was setting myself up for failure.

I knew it as soon as I walked into the tiny, sequestered room that we used for massage therapy. I had a tech on staff that I could very easily call to handle this for me. That would be the smart thing to do, the professional thing, but I wasn't going to make the call.

Nope, I was going to walk in that room with a naked Dominic Voss laid out on the table in front of me and torture myself by putting my hands all over the miles and miles of thick and ropey muscles that covered his big body, knowing that it couldn't lead to anything. Well knowing that it shouldn't lead to anything, but my self-control felt paper thin and stretched as tautly as it had ever been. I couldn't recall a point in my life where attraction had clawed at me, gnawed on my insides like a hungry monster demanding to be fed. It was hard to concentrate on anything else with ravenous need pulsing inside of me. I was tempting more than fate by going into that room and putting my hands on Dom, but I had reached the point that I no longer cared.

He was lying facedown on the table and he didn't look up when I entered the sage-scented room. The new age music that was typically piped in for relaxation was turned off, so the only sounds that filled the tiny space were the alternate sounds of both of our heavy breathing. His sounded like he was getting ready to fall asleep. Mine sounded like I had just run a marathon. His hair was damp from his shower and I took a moment to silently chastise myself for being so caught up in my own thoughts that I hadn't bothered to spruce myself up after the sweaty yoga session. All I did was throw on a white T-shirt and muck around in the mire of my wayward thoughts. I probably smelled like the floor of the gym, but there wasn't any time to fix it or worry about it now.

I made sure the door clicked shut behind me so that he knew I was in the room, but he still didn't move. I wondered if he actually had fallen asleep. I cleared my throat a little bit and told him, "I'm going to focus mostly on your shoulder to see if we can get that muscle to loosen back up. It probably won't feel all that great at the beginning and you need to make sure you hydrate when we're done."

My voice was huskier than it typically was and I had to shake my head at myself. I needed to get it together so I could do my job and get him out of here without making a fool of myself. I picked up the bottle of oil infused with different essential oils and approached the table. I almost jumped when he finally turned his head, which was directly in line with my crotch and looked up at me with knowing shining out of his olive-green eyes. "Do your worst."

I sucked in a sharp breath at the blatant challenge and told my dick to behave considering its close proximity to his smirking mouth. I rubbed my hands together to warm the oil up and when I put them on his skin we both jolted at the initial contact. I'd had my hands on bodies worth millions, on ones that were sculpted and honed to perfection, ones that belonged to men that made it no secret that I could get away with much more than a massage in this private little space. None of them made me react the way Dominic did.

As soon as I touched him I knew I was never going to want to stop. I wanted to memorize every muscle, trace every dip, explore every hollow and lick my way across every inch of his golden skin. It was consuming and I felt like I was drowning under endless layers of want and need. My dick was no longer listening and had taken on a life of its own. Rock hard and throbbing, the straining erection that was now pushing against the too-thin fabric of my shorts was very aware of how close it was to Dom's mouth as he breathed in and out in a steady rhythm.

I dug my fingers into the coiled muscle of his shoulder and winced along with him when I found the tangled knot of tendons and ligaments that he had overworked during the weekend. He hissed out a sound of pain and I had to bite back a groan as the heat of it wafted over the tip of my cock. This was such a terrible and fantastic idea.

"I told you it was going to hurt a little bit." I used my thumbs and really dug in using a circular motion and the skin and muscle gave under the pressure. I knew he wouldn't openly complain no matter how uncomfortable he was so I had to make sure that I tempered my touch and didn't hurt him more than he already was.

He snorted and peeled an eye open, but this time kept his gaze focused on the part of my body that was practically begging him for attention.

"Looks like I'm not the only one hurting a little bit." There were equal amounts of humor and sex laced throughout his tone and it took a Herculean effort on my part to keep moving my hands and to keep focused on the task at hand.

It wasn't just the knot in his shoulder that was tense and hard. He was solid through and through, pretty much just tight skin stretched over miles of muscle that had very little give. He was in better shape than a lot of the athletes that I worked on. It was another indicator of how serious he was about his job and taking on the role of hero. A man didn't get a body like Dom's without serious effort and dedication. Everything he did was tied into him being a police officer and even with the evidence of that, tactile and real, under my fingertips, I still wanted him.

I wanted to get to know him. I wanted to see if his brash and flirty nature extended all the way to the bedroom, and I wanted to know if he did everything else as well as he kissed. I wanted to spend time with him outside of this gym and I wanted to let myself want him.

We both tensed and seemed to stop breathing as I moved the rest of the way down his back and lifted the sheet that covered his lower half. I purposely skipped putting my hands anywhere near the almost perfect ass that was staring me in the face and went to work on his injured leg. I was surprised to find it crisscrossed in various surgical scars and ridged with scar tissue. I hadn't seen this much of him uncovered before considering that he usually wore track pants or sweats when we met for his sessions. I felt him tense as I absently traced my fingers over the brutal marks that were stark and pale against his dark skin.

"You have a very dangerous job, Dominic." The words rushed out before I could stop them and I knew they sounded accusatory, but I couldn't help it.

His thigh muscle twitched and I heard him sigh. "I do. But how many clients do you see that are hurt worse than I am that aren't in law enforcement, Lando?"

He had a valid point. Some of my hardest cases came off the field or were the results of traffic accidents that had nothing to do with the kind of danger he faced every day. I didn't answer as I used my palms to work the long muscles in his legs. The gesture made his ass cheeks clench under the sheet covering his hips and I heard him groan. I wasn't sure if it was in pleasure or pain, but my guess would be the first. I wanted to groan, too. He really was a sight to behold, laid out before me like he was.

By the time I got to his other leg and was about to tell

him to turn over so that I could torture myself by working on the front of him, Dom had had enough. He flipped over on the table and sat up.

He reached out and grabbed one of my oil-slicked hands in his. His dark eyebrows were low over his eyes and there was no missing the veritable tent at the front of the sheet where it barely covered him or the heat in his gaze as he told me, "Okay, there is only one place on the front of me I want your hands, so you need to let me know right now if you're on board with that or not. If not I'm going to very carefully get up off this table and go home."

I exhaled so hard my nostrils flared out. I felt a little dizzy and my thoughts between what I should say to him and what I was going to say to him were banging so loudly into one another it made my head hurt . . . but not as bad as my throbbing dick hurt.

"I'm on board. I shouldn't be, but I am." I blinked at him for a second and then shook my head ruefully. "If I put my hands on your dick you're going to have to work with a different PT, Dom."

His eyebrows shot up and a wicked grin pulled at him mouth. I wanted to kiss it off him. "Then find me another PT to work with and put your hands on my dick and come closer so I can put my mouth on yours." I wasn't really sure if he meant put his mouth on my dick or my mouth, but really I was okay with it being on either so I took a step forward.

It was a monumental step. I went from falling to actively leaping into the unknown with someone that scared the hell out of me and the thrill of it popped and zinged up and down my spine in a rush.

I reached the edge of the table and put a hand on his shoulder. I figured I could lead up to getting to the good stuff, but I already knew Dom was the impatient type, so it didn't shock me at all when he took that hand off his shoulder and put it directly on his very eager and very erect cock. It jumped as soon as my fingers curled around the thickness and I let out a little moan as his hand slipped around the back of my head and pulled me down until our open mouths lined up. It was his turn to kiss me.

It was less desperate and frantic than the kiss I had laid on him in the parking lot. He was more in control than I had been and I liked the push and pull of us against each other. I also liked the way his entire body tensed up and moved towards mine as I started to move my hand up and down the turgid shaft. It made my own arousal tighten and pulse in time to his rapid heartbeat.

Our tongues tangled. Our chests pressed together. Our hands got anxious and grabby and our breath rushed in and out as we pressed closer and closer into one another. Dom's hips kicked up off the massage table as the flat of my palm rolled over the sensitive tip of his cock. He was already leaking and quivering like it wouldn't take much to push him over the edge and I liked the shot of satisfaction that gave me. I was all about making people feel good and when it was someone I wanted naked and all over me then I took extra pride in their pleasure. And god damn, did pleasure look good on Dom.

It made him a little more rugged, a shade rougher, a hint more jagged than he already was and fuck if it wasn't sexy as all hell. I tightened my grip even harder around him and started to pump my fist in earnest as he pulled back from the ravenous kiss and watched me with widened eyes. I normally had a pretty delicate touch, but something about him brought out the more daring side of my nature. It was an unbelievable turn-on to watch my much paler fist work his hardened and straining flesh. We both seemed mesmerized by the motion and he made a strangled sound low in his throat as he started to reach for the very tented front of my shorts.

I shook my head at him and lowered my head a little so I could kiss him again. This time there was a little bite behind it. "Not yet. Just watch."

He was panting now in short and choppy breaths as we both zeroed in on my hand moving on him up and down as his hips occasionally bucked up to meet the downward slide of my fist. He was damp and shiny from both the oil that was already on my hands and his own excitement. I couldn't recall ever seeing anything sexier. I wanted him in my mouth and inside my body. I wasn't so sure about his welcome inside my heart yet, considering we didn't know each other that well, but I could feel him knocking on the door.

He muttered a few dirty words and wrapped his hand around my wrist and squeezed as I buried my nose in the curve of his neck. I could feel his pulse jumping and skittering erratically against the tip of my tongue as I licked the long vein that throbbed just under his skin.

"If you don't want this to be a solo show you better let up and let me get my hands on the goods, Mr. Fancy-Pants."

The nickname was ridiculous considering the compromising situation we were currently in with one another so I sank my teeth into the side of his neck in a little nip and shook his hold off so I could finish the job I started. His already tight abs turned rock hard and those thick thigh muscles started to shake a little. I used the pad of my thumb to rub circles under the edge of the very sensitive head of his cock and we both gasped a little when his body bowed up and stream upon stream of hot pleasure rushed out and coated both of us. It was brilliant and bright and even without letting him lay a hand on me I was more turned on then I could ever remember being. Dom took me out of my comfort zone, and I knew all about the benefits of stretching before getting down to any actual work.

I lifted my head up from where I was still nuzzling his neck and let go of his now softening member. I wanted to touch the evidence of how well I had handled him where it was dotting his delineated abs but before I could get a word out or make another move towards him he was using the edge of the sheet to clean himself off as he swung his legs to the side and got to his feet.

He loomed in front of me like a darkly satisfied warrior and started to advance on me. He was naked and loose from the orgasm, but the look in his eyes was focused and determined as he prowled towards me as I involuntarily took a step back. I took another and another until my back hit the door and Dom was right in front of me and in my face. His breath was hot as he leaned up until he could growl directly into my ear, "You always seem to be handling me, Orlando. In one way or another you are the one calling the shots. I've got some shots of my own I want to take."

I wasn't going to argue, but I wouldn't have gotten the chance if I was. His mouth was back on mine and he was pulling my T-shirt up and over my head within the span of a second. His lips were hard and left little doubt that he was serious about getting more than his hands all over me for a change of pace. I sighed lightly into his mouth as our tongues twisted together and his hands started to roam over my now bare chest. As big and as forceful as he often came across, his touch was surprisingly light and way more reverent and delicate than mine had been with him. It took me a second to realize he was taking the time to brush his fingers over each and every single freckle that dotted my skin. There were a lot of them so by the time he got to the ones below my bellybutton I was kiss drunk and sex stupid.

I wanted to grab his head and force him to his knees in front of me. I could tell he knew it, too. He was grinning at me, which was extra sexy with his mouth red and shiny from being all over mine.

He slipped a finger into the elastic band at the top of my shorts and tugged just enough to let the tip of my dick peek out. He lifted an eyebrow at the ruddy tip and his grin turned downright wicked.

"I want to see how far down your freckles go." His

voice rumbled out of his chest and the deep rasp of it made my skin pebble in anticipation.

I wheezed a little when he finally lowered himself to the floor in front of me, taking my shorts down with him.

"I pretty much have them everywhere." When I was younger, I hated them because I felt like they were just one more thing that set me apart from the rest of the guys my age. Now I had grown into them and I kind of liked them. Dom was apparently a fan.

He chuckled and moved across my cock, which was practically leaping out to make his acquaintance. "I can see that. I like them. I want to connect them all with my tongue."

"Jesus." He laughed again as I let my head fall back against the door with a loud *thunk* at the first swipe of his tongue across the already leaking tip of my cock. "I don't know if I could survive that."

I looked down at him right as he leaned forward to wrap a hand around the base of my erection at the same time he surrounded the rest of the waiting length with the heat of his mouth. It was my turn to swear as my vision went cloudy around the edges and my knees went a little weak. I'd had plenty of guys go down on me back in my fuck-to-forget days, but nothing felt like Dom's mouth on me. It obliterated thought. It killed common sense. It annihilated any hesitation I had about throwing myself in with this man. His mouth on me, his hand twisting in time with the motion of his bobbing head, felt like it *had* to happen. It felt better than any blow job had a right to feel. It felt more intense and involved than the last time I had actual sex with someone. It felt fated and destined. I couldn't tear my eyes away from his as he looked up at me with a perceptive glint in his eye.

I told myself to breathe because things were getting fuzzy and I felt lightheaded. I curled one hand around the back of his dark head and let his short hair tickle the tips of my fingers as I urged him to go farther and farther down. I wanted him to take as much of me as he could and he obliged without so much as blinking an eye. I put my other hand over my heart and tried to hold it in as it threatened to beat its way out of my chest. The intensity of it all was going to take me to the ground.

He made a pleased sound around the rigid flesh in his mouth and I couldn't watch him anymore. I theoretically should have been the one in power, in control as I stood over him as he swallowed me back as far in his throat as he could. But it was all Dom. He was the one in charge as he worked me over and handled me like I was made of clay. I was pliable in his hands, willing to let him do whatever he wanted, and what he wanted was to make me come undone as quickly as possible.

I swore again as his free hand, which had been hovering over his own reawakening erection, suddenly appeared between my legs and wrapped around my overly sensitive sac. The caress had my eyes flying back open and my fingers digging into his scalp. He rolled his palm over the delicate skin and pleasure throbbed so hard at the base of my spine at the skilled touch, it almost hurt.

"Dominic . . ." I gasped his name out as a warning that

I was close to the point of no return and he made a hum-ming noise that shot all the way through my dick and into my gut. I groaned and then jolted as his hand left my balls and skipped up between my legs, along the curve of my ass and dipped into places I wasn't sure I was ready to let him touch yet.

Whether I was ready or not didn't matter to Dom as the tip of his finger teased the tight and hidden place.

I said his name, but it was broken and torn from my throat. It was all the warning he got before my body rebelled and gave into the rampaging pleasure he was coaxing from it. I panted, shallow and ragged breaths as I curled both my hands around the sides of his head and held him still as I danced and dripped desire all across the surface of his tongue.

His eyes were alive with self-satisfaction and pride as he wrung me out to dry and left me slumped, weak and boneless, against the door. It was an unfamiliar feeling. I'd never handed myself over to someone else like that before. Not even with Remy. With him, everything had been a gentle exploration, a discovery of what love and forever should feel like. With Dom, it felt like I was al-ready at the top of the mountain and ready to jump off. It was the exhilaration of the battle won and the fear of the unknown crashing that amplified every touch and every shared breath. He pulled back and kissed the center of my stomach, which had the muscles pulling tight.

He went to get back up to his feet and halted before he got halfway up as his bad leg betrayed him. His face pulled tight in a wince of pain as I reached out and helped him up. We stood facing each other naked and as exposed as we could be.

He lifted a hand and rubbed it over the surface of his short hair and gave me a rueful grin. "Maybe I should have let you focus on the other muscles that needed your attention after all. Those aren't such an easy fix."

I cleared my throat and situated myself back inside my shorts. "I'm not sure anything about any of this is easy."

He rolled his heavy shoulders and turned to walk over to the hooks on the wall that held his discarded clothes. "Most things that are easy aren't worth much. It's the things you have to work for that matter the most."

I cleared my throat again. "I'll keep that in mind." And I would, because "easy" was not a word that I would ever associate with Dominic Voss, and how I was starting to feel about him was anything but.

Chapter Seven

Dominic

THE CALL CAME in as I was headed out the door to go to my first physical therapy session with a trainer that wasn't Lando. I was walking down the stairs of my apartment building and headed towards my car when Royal's boyfriend's name flashed across the screen of my phone. I contemplated ignoring it and him but figured he wouldn't be calling me unless it was something important like our girl had locked herself out of somewhere again and I was closer to ride to the rescue.

I was so used to Asa's slow, mellow southern drawl that when his words came out in a rush I had a hard time deciphering what he was trying to tell me. The bits and pieces I did pick out, like "accident," "hurt," "emergency room," and "unconscious" made my heart lodge in my throat and the world tilt dangerously off-kilter. I had to grab the handrail on the stairs because I momentarily lost my balance and almost ended up on my ass.

I asked Asa if he had called Royal's mother and he just grunted at me and bit out a harsh, "No." I told him I would make the call since there seemed to be some kind of hostility on his end towards my best friend's flighty parent. Royal's mom wouldn't ever be inducted into the parenting hall of fame, but they were close and she was going to want to be there if Royal was hurt, even if it meant facing the silent scorn that seemed to emanate off of Asa when she was around. He told me what hospital they were at and I jogged the rest of the way down the stairs, calling not only Royal's mom but my own as I did so. She would want to know what was going on with the young woman she loved like one of her own as well.

The call to Royal's mom was exhausting and frustrating. The woman was as dramatic as they came and since I didn't have any details I couldn't ease her fears or hysterics as she started screaming, "My baby! I told her she was going to get hurt!" over and over again. Finally, I couldn't handle it anymore and just hung up on her. She was going to have to pull her shit together before she showed up at the hospital. I had a feeling Asa wouldn't let her anywhere near Royal unless she showed up in full-on mom mode, something that was always a struggle for the woman.

My own mother took the news more stoically and asked if I wanted her to meet me at the emergency room. I told her to hold off until I had more information and promised to keep her updated when I knew more. She was worried but not one to fly off the handle like Royal's mom, and the calm assurance did wonders to slow my rapidly thundering heart. I wasn't going to assume the worst. I couldn't.

When I got to the hospital, I moved as fast as I was able to since my own accident. I was intimately familiar with the emergency wing of the hospital, so it took me no time at all to maneuver my way through the sterile halls and around scrub-clad staff in the halls. Asa was easy enough to spot as soon as I hit the waiting room and intake area. He was standing by the desk talking to a lovely redheaded woman dressed in scrubs. Asa was a charmer and a stupidly attractive man. He seemed to attract female attention wherever he went, but the time and the place were not right for him to be flirting. It made me narrow my eyes at the scene before me.

The nurse had a hand on the outside of his arm and was looking up at him in a way that seemed way more personal than professional. There was concern and sympathy stamped on every line of her expressive face and I could see that she was trying to comfort the tall, blond southerner the best she could. He would nod occasionally at whatever it was she was telling him and at one point he reached down and enfolded the woman in a hug, which made my back teeth clench together. His girlfriend was injured, supposedly unconscious somewhere in this hospital, and he had the nerve to have his hands on the first pretty face that wandered by? I wanted to choke him and then kick him.

The redheaded nurse returned the hug, said some-

thing else to him and then picked up a chart and disappeared down the labyrinth of hallways, giving me my
opening to approach. Asa turned just as I reached him
and his whiskey-colored eyes widened in shock as I put
my hands on the center of his chest and gave him a solid
shove. He fell back a step and caught himself on the edge
of the desk where he had been snuggling with the nurse
a moment ago.

"Royal is hurt and you're already lining up her re-
placement? I told you if you broke her heart again I was
going to break you." The words snapped out harsh and
fast, fueled by worry and anger.

Asa held his hands up and then moved them to shove
back his sandy hair. "That nurse is engaged to one of my
closest friends in case you missed the sparkler on her
finger." He lifted his tawny eyebrows at me. "She also
used to live across the hall from Royal and considers her
her best friend, so she's just as worried as you and I are.
Something you would know if you bothered to meet the
new people in her life, Dom."

I winced. He had a point. When I got hurt, Royal had
spiraled down into a dangerous depression and it wasn't
me that stopped her fall. It was her new group of friends,
and this man that had been there for her without fail. I
hadn't made any kind of effort to meet them because it
was a painful reminder that life and all the people I loved
most in it moved on, grew, changed, while I was stuck just
waiting to see if my body would heal. Everyone was going
forward and I was stuck on pause. I hated it and kind of
resented that while I couldn't do anything about my situ-

ation, Royal's life had become so full and vibrant. If I had been thinking clearly I probably would have put two and two together and realized the nurse was her friend Saint that Royal talked about pretty much all the time.

I grumbled a weak apology that Asa graciously accepted. "What happened? Did she get hurt at work?" I was picturing a high-speed chase gone wrong, or a desperate suspect ramming into her patrol car trying to flee the scene of the crime.

Asa shook his head and heaved a deep sigh. "She was driving home from the grocery store and a kid texting ran a red light and T-boned her right on the driver's side. The Four-Runner flipped, but she had her seat belt on, thank God." He rubbed his hands over his face and I could see the pain and worry bright in his gaze. "She was in and out of consciousness at the scene, so they brought her in and rushed her in for a CT scan. Other than that, she got a wicked gash on her arm from broken glass and was complaining that it hurt to breathe, so she might have a couple busted ribs. Saint said she would come and let me know when they move her back into a room after the scan." He blew out a breath and lifted a hand to rub the back of his neck. "I don't think I've ever been so scared in my life, when Saint called and said there was an accident and that Royal was being rushed in."

I nodded a little and felt some of the resentment I had towards this man that held my best friend's heart in his hands fade. "I felt the same way when you called me. I automatically thought it had something to do with work."

He swore under his breath. "Yeah. I worry about that

call all the time, too, but it's what she does, so it's just part of loving her."

That was surprisingly understanding, and I was starting to really see what Royal saw in this man aside from his obvious physical appeal.

"I called her mom. So she will be putting in an appearance at some point in time." I watched as his jaw involuntarily clenched.

"Thanks for the warning." He sounded like I had just told him the world was going to end and he was going to have to sit dockside and watch it all happen.

I wasn't exactly a fan of Royal's mom either, but there was something more to why Asa seemed to flat-out despise her. I wanted to ask about it, but I figured it could wait for another time. The pretty redheaded nurse was walking back towards us and this time there was no missing the sparkling diamond on her left ring finger. It wasn't flashy or ostentatious but it was there and I felt like a total tool and a really shitty cop for not being more observant and getting all the facts before attacking Asa.

"She's back in the room. She had a pretty ugly concussion that they want to keep under observation for a little bit and she's gonna need pain meds for that cut on her arm. She's probably going to want to follow up with a plastic surgeon."

I blinked. "It's that bad?"

The woman turned the softest, kindest gray eyes I had ever seen in my direction and looked at me quizzically.

Asa motioned between us. "Saint Ford, meet the elusive Dominic Voss, and might I say it's about fucking time." His twang was anything but sweet when he said it.

The redhead took a step forward and I thought she was going to reach for my hand, so I was stunned when she went right around the extended offering and went right in for a hug. I had to admit when her arms wrapped around my waist I felt a little better.

"Uh . . . nice to meet you, Saint."

It sounded like she sniffled a little into my chest, so I patted her on the back. She pulled away from me and her eyes were indeed glassy with unshed tears when she looked up at me. "It's nice to meet you, too, Dominic. I feel like I already know you. Royal talks about you all the time, and I was here the night they brought you in. Well, here but not on duty. I remember the trauma team thinking the prognosis wasn't all that great, so I'm so happy to see you up and around." She cleared her throat a little and turned to look back at Asa. "She's got two broken ribs and a few that are really, really bruised. She's not going to be moving around much the next few weeks."

He nodded. "I'll take care of her."

She gave him a little grin. "I know you will, but if she needs anything I want you to call me." She sighed and shook her head a little. "The kid that hit her didn't get off so lucky. He snapped a couple vertebrae in his neck and spine. He's lucky to be alive, but his careless act is going to have lifelong consequences. It's sad, he's so young."

She gave us directions to the room they had Royal in and told Asa that she would check in on her friend before they discharged her. Asa and I silently made our way to the unit, both stiff with tension but maybe just maybe feeling a little stronger that we were facing the unknown together.

I let him go into the room first and almost ran into his broad back as he came to a sudden stop in front of me. I nudged him and when he moved so that he could reach the edge of Royal's bed, I saw what had shocked him still.

Royal looked ravaged and battered. Like a fragile, broken toy all wrapped up in bandages and covered in black and blue marks. Her face was a startling grayish tone, which only enhanced the twin black circles around her eyes and the nasty gash that had little white strips of tape holding it shut over one of her eyebrows. The arm that was injured was swathed up like a mummy where it was poking out of her hospital gown and I could see the purple mark on her collarbone that the impact and jolt against the seat belt had left.

"If it isn't my two favorite guys." Her words were barely a whisper and I could see how much pain she was in just trying to get them out.

Asa bent down and clasped her good hand in his as he pressed his lips to the top of her head. I saw him close his eyes and whisper something to her that I couldn't hear. Whatever it was had tears shining in Royal's eyes and her squeezing his fingers.

"I guess I finally have to get a new car." I knew she said it as a joke, but I couldn't even smile at her. I felt like I was frozen on the spot, helpless and ineffective while she lay there hurt and damaged. I had a startling realization that this was probably exactly how she felt after my accident.

"Jesus, Royal. You scared the shit out of me. I almost fell down the stairs when Asa called me and told me what happened."

She blinked her watery eyes at me as I took the steps needed to reach the other side of her hospital bed. The corner of her mouth quirked up. "I know the feeling, hero."

I blew out a pent-up breath. "I know you do. How about we make a pact to stay out of the emergency room from here on out?"

I held out my hand with just my pinky finger sticking out. She let go of Asa's hand long enough to hook her own pinkie around mine as I gently moved them up and down.

"We can sure try." Her tone indicated that considering we both had a dangerous jobs the likelihood of that happening was slim. My gut kicked as I realized she was probably right . . . well, would be if I could get myself back on the force.

"I had Dom call your mom so she should be here shortly." She looked up at Asa and some silent couple communication happened that I was completely left out of. I wasn't used to Royal having secrets from me and I didn't like it.

I glowered at them both and crossed my arms over my chest. "Someone want to let me in on why it's such a big deal to have your boyfriend and mother in the same room, especially considering the circumstances?"

Royal went to shrug and then shouted out in pain. Asa put a hand on her shoulder and cut me a dark look. "Roslyn and I don't see eye to eye on a lot of things where her relationship with Royal is concerned. I prefer not to be in the same room with her, but that doesn't matter. What matters is getting Royal comfortable until I can take her home." His amber eyes glinted with a danger I knew he had in him but I had never seen. "I can play nice when I have to, cop."

Royal was looking at me with eyes that pleaded for me to just let it drop and because I loved her and she was hurt I decided to do just that.

I sighed and told her, "I met Saint. She seems very nice. I'm so happy you have a friend like that looking out for you."

She gave me a loose grin and lifted up the back of Asa's hand so that she could rub it against her bruised cheek. "You would like all the people I've let into my life, Dom. You just need to give them a chance."

I looked between the two of them and nodded solemnly. "Point taken."

I hung around until the doctor came in and offered her a mild painkiller for her injuries. They wanted her to stay for observation for the rest of the day, and it was clear Asa had things under control and that he was who she was going to turn to for comfort and help, as it should be. I offered to stay to be the buffer when Royal's mom showed, but Asa told me he could handle it and I was inclined to believe him. There didn't seem to be much the southern charmer couldn't handle. I didn't want to be impressed by a guy with a criminal record as long as my arm, but I was, and there was no denying the proof that was right in front of me that he would do anything and everything for my best friend. He might have her heart, but it was obvious it was a fair trade because Royal held his just as tightly.

It wasn't until I was in my truck and headed back towards my apartment building that I remembered I had somewhere else I was supposed to be that day. I tried to call Lando's cell phone and it went right to voice mail. I thought about going by the clinic but didn't want to interrupt him if he was with another client, so I called his cell back and left a rambling message about why I had missed my appointment. I didn't want him to get any ideas that it had anything to do with what had gone down between us during my last session.

When I pulled into my spot in front of my building, the sleek sports car that was parked in the spot next to it immediately caught my eye. So did the tall man holding a cup of Starbucks in his hand as he got out and made his way up to the sidewalk where I stopped to look at him.

"What are you doing here, Orlando?" I sounded as surprised as I felt.

He stopped before stepping on the curb, so for once I had a height advantage on him. "I was worried when you missed your appointment. Your new trainer called a couple of times and it went to voice mail."

I frowned and pulled out my phone. "I just called you and it went right to voice mail. Royal was in a car accident and she's in the hospital. I turned my phone off when I was in her room."

His expression pulled into one of instant concern. "Is she alright?"

"She's been better. Do you make house calls when all your clients are no-shows?" I wasn't sure why I felt the need to prod him, but I couldn't seem to stop myself. I never could with him.

He muttered something under his breath and I saw his long fingers tense around the white cup in his hand. "I was worried. About you. About us . . . I don't know. I've never stepped over the line with a client or a man like that before. I just wanted to make sure everything was okay."

His anxiousness was cute. He was cute, and I was really glad he was here. I never really had anyone else to lean on when shit went south. I was usually the pillar that held everyone else up.

"You and I are fine, Lando. In fact, you and I might be the only thing I can honestly say is A-OK at this point." I reached out a hand and put it on the side of his neck. A thrill shot through me as his pulse immediately leapt up to kiss my fingertips.

"It's been a pretty shitty day, so if you don't have to go back to work, why don't you come upstairs with me and we can get naked and do really fun and dirty things to one another?" I said it jokingly, but the way his light eyes sparked at the suggestion made me think there was nothing funny about the two of us getting naked together.

He hissed out a breath between his teeth and closed his eyes briefly. When they snapped open, I knew he was coming upstairs with me.

"I've got a few hours."

I chuckled. "That might be enough time. Let's find out."

Chapter Eight

Lando

IT FELT LIKE the most natural thing in the world to follow those wide shoulders up the stairs and into the darkened apartment. There was no doubt, no second thoughts, and I found myself wishing I didn't have to go back to work for my final client of the day.

When Dom had been a no-show for his appointment, all manner of the worst things that could have happened to him started running through my mind. I wondered if he had hurt himself again, if maybe our liaison hadn't left him as twisted up and anxious for a repeat as it had left me. He was assertive and flirty, but there was a chance that things had gone further than either of us intended and that made me panic on a personal and professional level. The last thing I wanted was my rampaging hormones where the hot cop was concerned to taint my reputation. The world was more open-minded than it had ever been, but I could only imagine the way some of my clients would react if they thought they were going to have to fend off my advances during a session.

My relief that there was a totally logical reason Dom hadn't shown was palpable and probably part of the reason I offered no resistance when he took my almost empty coffee cup from me and took my hand to guide me through the run-of-the-mill apartment towards what I assumed was his bedroom. The décor was very typical single-dude style. Heavy black furniture and lots of sleek electronics. There were pictures on the wall of him and two young women that looked so much like him that I knew they had to be his sisters. There were also pictures of him in his uniform with an attractive older woman that I assumed was his mom.

The sight of him dressed in his patrol uniform sent a surprising jolt of desire blasting through my system. I liked boys in uniform, but those uniforms usually involved bulky pads and tight football pants. I had no clue how sexy a man with a badge could be, not to mention the handcuffs.

He tugged on my hand when I stalled and turned to see what I was staring at. I tapped the picture that showed him a few years younger and actually smiling with his mother on one side and Royal on the other dressed exactly the same.

"You look good in uniform."

Both of his dark eyebrows winged up and a smile

slashed across his face. "I look better out of it. Come on, we've got a ticking clock working against us."

It was typically a few weeks or even months into dating before I found myself in a guy's room or welcomed them into mine. Before I got to this point there was usually the period of getting to know someone and learning what they liked, what they disliked, and if we were on equal footing when it came to expectations in the bedroom. Some guys were all about giving, some guys all about receiving, and then there were the few that considered sex a team sport and could get on board with either or. Dominic and I hadn't even been close to that kind of conversation, and yet I went willingly as he pulled me closer to him by the front of my shirt and placed a bruising kiss on my mouth. It was obvious he was on edge, as rough as he was, normally whenever he touched me he did so with care and this time there was none of that present.

I let him devour my mouth, nip at my lips and pull my shirt up and over my head. He was impatient and his hands were everywhere. His rush made me feel like I could actually hear the ticking of a clock as he put a hand in the center of my now bare chest and walked me backwards towards his unmade bed in the center of the room. All the while he continued to ravage my mouth like he was starving and I was the only way he could get any kind of sustenance.

I wrapped my hands around his rock-hard biceps to try and steady him and pulled back a little on a gasp as my lungs started to burn with the need for oxygen. I'd never been kissed like my lips were the answer to everything that was wrong in the world before and I had to admit it was a pretty intoxicating feeling.

I ran my hand over the curve of his shoulder and clasped the side of his face as he attacked my belt buckle and started to pull my hips towards him since I wasn't bending and sitting on the edge of the bed like he obviously wanted me to.

"Dom." I evaded his wicked and tempting lips as he leaned in for another kiss. "We should take a minute and talk."

His eyebrows slashed down over his celadon-colored eyes. Impatience made every line of his strong body tense as he pulled back and gave me a dark look. "A talk about what?"

I just stared at him because I thought it was obvious. I put my free hand on the other side of his face and leaned forward until our foreheads were touching. "About how we do this. I like you, Dom, and I think you like me. It would be a shame if we screwed that all up by not taking the time this thing between us feels like it deserves."

He let out a heavy breath and the weight of it across my parted lips was an entirely different kind of kiss.

"Is this the do you wanna fuck or get fucked talk?" It was so crude and blatant that it shocked a laugh out of me.

"Uh . . . yeah. Pretty much." I stilled as his hands slid around my naked waist and into the slack top of my pants so that they rested on the curve at the top of my ass.

"I don't care." He breathed the words out and I tasted their sincerity as they touched my lips.

"You don't care?" That was unusual and it raised a

flag of alarm. I wanted him to take what was happening between the two of us as seriously as I was. I moved my hands to his shoulders and pulled my head back so that we were looking at each other eye to eye. "How can you not care?"

He grunted at me and moved back so that he could pull his own shirt over his head. I was distracted momentarily by the flex and stretch of his toned torso.

"Sometimes I care. Depends on the guy and the situation. With you I don't care. I'm happy you're here so I'll take you any way I can get you."

That might be the most flattering thing anyone had ever said to me, and if he was down for whatever, then I could roll with that. I was kind of in the same frame of mind. As long as I got to have some part of him, I didn't really care about how I got it.

Now I was the one that was impatient and wanted him naked as fast as I could get him. I finally went backwards on the bed and went after his heavy silver belt buckle with fingers that seemed to have forgotten how to work. The task was made even more difficult as he bent over to finish the job he started by pulling my pants the rest of the way down my legs. In a matter of minutes, we were both in nothing more than our boxers. I was a cotton or silk kinda guy and it looked like Dom was a boxer brief man. They suited him, but they were in the way, so I reached out a finger and hooked the elastic at the top and tugged.

"You're right, you do look better out of uniform." He snorted at me, but it quickly turned into a sharply in-haled breath as I moved the fabric out of the way so that his waiting cock could fall into my eager hands. I curled my fingers around the width and gave the shaft a pump. His hips arched towards me so he leaned forward as I continued to move my fist up and down so that he was bent over me with a hand on the bed next to my head as I fell backwards.

"You look good in my bed, Mr. Fancy-Pants." His voice was raspy and it was my turn to struggle to breathe as his free hand skipped over the contours of my chest and disappeared into the waistband of my boxers. He freed my erection with a deft touch and rolled his thumb over the tip while I continued to work his shaft up and down with a firm grip.

I cocked an eyebrow and bent a knee to make more room for him between my legs. He seemed to be comfortable where he was, looming over me, looking down at me with heated eyes, so I saw no need to switch places. "I'm not wearing any pants, fancy or otherwise."

Dom chuckled and lowered his head so that our lips barely touched. The tip of his tongue darted out and licked the center of my top lip super softly. It was just the hint of a touch, the barest caress, and it was almost as sexy as the way his fingers were moving across my throbbing dick. "I know. It's a good look for you, Lando."

Heaving chest pressed into heaving chest while our mouths merged and our tongues tangled. We both made a strangled noise as hard cock brushed against hard cock the closer he leaned into me. He bent his elbow so that he was barely hovering over me, our stomachs touched and I liked that he felt so much bigger, so much heavier than anyone else ever had. He was substantial. He was significant . . . and so was the pleasure that coiled tight and urgent at the base of my spine as we each did our best to get the other off first.

It was a flurry of pumping hands, weeping tips, and bucking hips. Our bodies moved together and against each other kind of like they had been doing so for ages instead of minutes, and again I wondered how something so rash, so sudden and unexpected, could feel so necessary, so vital. There was no warning with Dominic Voss; there was just the drop and the fall into a swirling vortex of feeling and emotion and I was done trying to catch myself.

He moved his lips to the side of my neck and I moaned a guttural sound and arched up into him as his hot tongue started tracing the long line of vein and muscle that was stretched taut with pleasure as my straining cock swelled and pulsed eagerly into his talented touch. I was on the brink, ready to come, and I could feel the hitch in his breath and the kick in his turgid member that let me know he was close as well. I was going to move my hand lower, urge him to let go first when he levered up off of me, and suddenly let go of my begging dick and pulled his out of my exploring grasp.

I was about to demand he get back and finish what he started when I heard him rummaging around in a drawer on the nightstand next to the bed. I blinked when he was back, hovering over me with a condom in one hand and a familiar bottle of lubrication in the other. I blinked because he was so prepared, so ready, like having a guy show up at his apartment ready for sex was such a common occurrence that he had to have stuff on hand to make sure he got laid without a hitch. It made a sliver of unease slide through the passion and desire that was overriding everything else.

Some of my concern must have made its way onto my face because he stopped in the middle of suiting that mighty impressive erection up in the latex and cocked his head to the side as he looked at me.

"You okay?" He sounded genuinely concerned, so I propped myself up on my elbows and cast a look down at his waist and then back up at his questioning eyes.

"You just seem really prepared and I guess we don't really know that much about each other. I don't sleep around, Dom." My dick might murder me if he got freaked out by what I was saying and called a halt to our sexual escapades, but I had to be up front with what my expectations were. That was only fair to both of us.

Dom finished rolling the condom down his engorged shaft and gave the base a solid squeeze which made my mouth go dry. I could totally get on board with watching him get himself off. That sounded like a good time for all.

"I'm a cop, Lando. It's in my nature to be prepared for any circumstance that might arise. I don't sleep around either, but I have been single for a while now and on occasion I have met someone here or there I only want to spend a night with. You are not one of those guys."

It wasn't like I could pass any kind of judgment. There was a time not too long ago where I was only down to have a boy in my life for the night and as long as he was telling me that wasn't the case with us, I felt like I had to believe him. I wanted to believe him.

I gave him a little nod as he crooked his finger at me and told me to move closer to the edge of the bed with my legs bent. I took a deep breath and shifted into the position he requested. We locked eyes as he leaned over me and my very ready dick as his hand, now coated and slick, coiled around my cock and moved up and down at a languid pace. My breath hitched as he took his time, rolled over the tip and circled the head with a delicate touch before skating between my legs and rubbing over my taut sac.

My thigh muscles quivered, my abs pulled as tight as they had ever been as his firm touch disappeared between my legs and onto that spot that he needed to get ready for him. There was always the initial stretch and pull, and the tight ring of muscle got ready to yield. My heart kicked in my chest and I could see his nostrils flare as he worked a finger in and out of me while I struggled to keep my breathing in check.

Dom reached out with his free hand and picked up one of mine where it was lying on the bed. He put it on my now shiny and still straining erection and told me, "Touch yourself." It was all so overwhelmingly intimate. So unrestrained and uninhibited. Even when I had taken strangers to bed knowing good and well I would never see them again, I hadn't felt this same sense of freedom, of acceptance and approval. And while sex with Remy had always been sweet and heartfelt, full of emotion and sentiment, it had also been plagued by newness, doubt, and uncertainty. There was never this level of comfort, of rightness, with anyone else and I didn't even know Dom's middle name, or his favorite color, or what his favorite band was. It was all a little disconcerting and again I got the feeling of being cut off at the knees and leveled to the ground by this man.

Dom pulled away just enough that he could brace a hand on the bed right next to my hip as he used the other one to line himself up with my waiting body. He wasn't a small guy and I knew it was going to be a tight fit, but the burn and the ache as he slowly slid inside did nothing to lessen the grip pleasure had on all of my senses. His dark head was bent low as he watched not only himself going in and out of me, but also me as I continued to rub my fist up and down my dick which was now thumping against his lower stomach each time he sank inside of me as far as he could go.

He groaned my name as my body instinctively tightened around him as he started to move faster and faster. He was big and strong so he had to place a hand on my hip to keep me anchored to the side of the bed so that his powerful thrusts didn't shift me away from the position he wanted me in.

I was pinned, immobilized and very full of Dom. I don't think there was any better place I could ever ask to be.

I felt my breath quicken and desire start to curl up all the way from my toes. My hand moved faster on my dick and my balls drew up even tighter against my body. Dom's eyes glowed with a minty green I hadn't seen yet and his teeth sank into the curve of his lower lip.

"You're close." The roughness of his voice as it struggled to make its way out was its own kind of sexy caress.

"I am." I was panting and my hips were shifting involuntarily as he continued to pound into me like he wanted to put me through the other side of the bed. I loved the feel of him, the stretch and pull that I had to do in order to take all of him. It was sex that would leave its mark, would leave a memory in more ways than one.

"Good, because I'm not going to last much longer." He dropped his head and growled low in his throat as he shifted the hand he had on my hip so that he could palm my tense balls while I continued to pump up and down on my cock. It was primal. It was raw. It was so real that it was all I needed to let go. There was no resisting the dual stimulation and the hard dick rapidly moving in and out of my body.

Pleasure rushed forth, spurted out and covered both our hands. Dom growled again, thrust his hips a couple more times, and then said my name like it was a wish come true. He groaned from deep in his chest as I watched all his muscles quake and shiver with satisfaction.

He sighed heavily, pulled out of me, and after dropping a quick kiss on the center of my chest right next to where my heart was trying to catch up with us, he flopped down next to me on the bed on his back so that we were both supine with our legs dangling over to the floor. We were both covered in sex and sweat. It should have been awkward or maybe a little uncomfortable but again it felt like the most natural thing in the world.

"I have tickets to the Avalanche game this weekend.

Do you want to go with me?" I blurted it out with zero finesse or tact. I didn't even know if he was a sports fan.

Dom blinked those army-green-colored eyes and that mouth I wanted all over me again quirked up in a half grin. "The best sex ever and tickets to an Aves game? You can't be for real."

I cleared my throat. "I am very real."

He tilted his chin up and winked at me. "Sure. I'd love to go with you, but I'd also like to put the rest of the time we have before you have to go back to work to good use."

It was my turn to grin at him. "I aim to please."

He sat up and reached over for my hand. "Good. Let's take a shower and switch places."

I could do that. I could also very easily let this man end up meaning everything to me, and the last time I had done that I had lost everything. I wanted Dom. I wanted what he had to offer, but I also wanted to keep my heart safe.

Chapter Nine

Dominic

I was struggling to keep things light and not too intense with Lando because I could tell every time that I was still going back to work was mentioned a change occurred in his demeanor. I was working with a new therapist, a young woman that cut me no slack and was just as tough on me about overdoing things as Lando had been. But even though I was with her 90 percent of the time during therapy, he still checked on me throughout the session and he had spent the last two nights in my apartment and in my bed. As long as the future wasn't brought up and I avoided any mention of what was next, things were great, but as soon as any hint of what was to come entered the equation, Lando got quite pensive and withdrawn. I knew he thought my job was dangerous and risky, that I was putting myself on the line with little reward for my effort, but it was what I did. It was who I was, and as much as I liked the guy, really liked him and could see something real and lasting happening between us, I wasn't going to give up everything in order to be with him. I couldn't. If I wasn't a cop I didn't know who I was and that shook me in ways I couldn't get my head around.

When the night of the game rolled around, I was really pumped. Not just because Lando had seats right on center ice behind the glass but because when I went to the gun range to see how training my non-dominant side to lead was coming along, I hit every target dead center and had no trouble loading and unloading the clip with my left hand. The recoil and jerk didn't even bother my shoulder, which was a first. Taking it easy on my body and making it stronger the right way was paying off and I could hardly contain my excitement.

I texted Royal first and got back a smiley face because she was still in a lot of pain from her ribs and just as annoyed as I had been about being laid up and unable to return to work until medically cleared. I texted Lando, too, and didn't get a response for well over an hour. I told myself that was because he was with a client and didn't have his phone on him, but deep down I knew that wasn't the case. He wasn't excited for me or happy about the news because it meant I was one step closer to getting my spot back on the force.

Eventually, I got back a smiley face from him as well with a message stating that he was excited to see me later that night. It burned a little. I wanted to be involved with him, wanted to let myself get attached, but something in the back of my mind warned it wasn't a good idea, that as soon as I was back on the streets, Lando would be nothing more than a fond memory. It was hard as hell to heal my body after it had been so badly broken, I didn't want to think about how impossible it would be to heal my heart if it ended up shattering on me. I decided my best bet was to keep things fun and sexy and just see where they took me. It was easier said than done when every single part of me leapt and pulsated with excitement and anticipation when he texted a few hours later to tell me he was waiting outside.

I was into him. Really into him, and it was going to suck when one of us had to walk away.

Those were worries for another day. All I was going to do was live in the moment and meet him as he leaned across the center console of his fancy-ass sports car for a kiss. A kiss that quickly had my blood heating and the interior of the car feeling smaller than it was. I liked it a lot when he wrapped his hand around the back of my head and scratched his nails along the scruff of my shaved head. This man understood what I liked and what was bound to make me react with a skill that shouldn't be possible in the short time we had known each other.

When I pulled back, we were both breathing hard and his freckles were standing out against the flush on his cheeks. I liked that he was as affected by me as I was by him.

I cleared my throat and asked, "How was work?"

He backed the sports car out of the space in front of

my building and replied like we weren't breathing hard and suffocating in sexual tension. "Work was good. I took on a disabled vet that was injured by an IED a few years ago. Someone recommended me and I think I can really help him. He needs to learn how to use his prosthetics properly because he hasn't been."

"Wow. That's a pretty big deal." I knew that he was all about helping people and stopping them from hurting any way he could, but I didn't realize how wide and deep that savior streak of his went. It was just as ingrained in him to help others as it was in me.

He shrugged. "Sometimes people that are injured become nothing more than their injuries. They end up defined by their limitations and what once was. I like to think I can show them there is always a new normal." His light eyes shifted to me and a smile that was definitely laced with sadness flashed at me. "You've done a pretty spectacular job of adjusting to your new normal."

My new normal was starting to revolve around him and having him in my life. "I couldn't have done any of it without you. You know that."

The car shipped through the downtown streets in a much more elegant and subdued way than my big truck attacked them. I wondered what he did when there was snow and ice on the ground. Sports cars were pretty and fun but totally impractical for four to five months out of the year in Denver.

"You have more determination than anyone I've ever met. You would have found your way to your new normal with or without me, Dom. I'm glad your journey brought us together, but you could have walked the path to recovery with anyone and ended up right where you want to be. Your fight to reach your destination has never wavered."

I cleared my throat a little and looked out the window as the Pepsi Center and all the maroon and blue lights that lit it up for the game came into view.

"The destination may have stayed the same throughout, but the path I've taken on my way there has plenty of room for detours and alternate routes." I shifted my attention to the big domed building. "I've never seen a hockey game live before. I'm gonna have to force myself to stay in my seat and not jump on the ice to break up all those fights." I grinned at him to let him know I was kidding, but he didn't grin back. Instead, he ran his hands through his hair and I saw him having some kind of internal conversation with himself. Whatever he was saying must have worked, because he gave his head a shake and reached for the driver's side door while looking at me over his shoulder.

"Are you a sports guy? I mean I assumed you were since you're in such good shape and you accepted my offer to come to the game so fast, but you've never mentioned anything about any of the athletes that come in and out of the clinic."

We walked towards the entrance shoulder to shoulder, my leather jacket rubbing against the arm of his wool pea coat as I contemplated his question. "I like sports. I played baseball when I was in high school, but that was more about my mom telling me I needed an activity than any real passion for the sport. I watch the Broncos play because my dad was a fan and I like football enough that I try and catch a game at the stadium at least once a year. Hockey is cool, but I don't know enough to tell you players' stats and rankings." I shrugged. "I stay in shape because bad guys will take whatever advantage they have and use it against you. I try to stay smarter, stronger, and faster than most of the people running the streets." I looked over at him. "What about you? You have an office filled with memorabilia and you said your dad was a recruiter but no pictures of you in a uniform."

He shrugged, which rubbed our arms together. I wondered how that little, unintentional touch could fire up my blood more effectively than a full-on hand on my dick. It was him. There was just something about Orlando Frederick that did it for me on every single level.

"I was always a sports guy. Growing up in a house with my dad, I didn't have much of a choice. But I loved it. I played soccer, I swam competitively, and I played lacrosse in college." He laughed a little and turned to look at me with humor stamped all across his face. "I even tried rugby for a while, but I wasn't built for it. You, on the other hand"—he lifted an eyebrow at me with a smirk—"you look like you were born to be in a scrum. If the whole law-enforcement thing doesn't work out, that can be your backup plan."

I think he was kidding but considering I knew how he felt about my job, I wasn't so sure. The image of that snapshot of him with his arm around the beautiful dark-haired boy dressed in a football uniform flashed behind my eyes.

"What about football? That not your cup of tea?" We sidestepped a couple arguing after I gave the guy a "watch yourself" look and lined up in the shortest line for the VIP ticket holders.

"I used to love football. It was my favorite sport. Right before I started college I had big plans to go into this field with the idea that I could be a team trainer. I had the connections thanks to my dad, but . . ." He trailed off as we moved forward and handed our tickets to the guy in the yellow staff jacket manning the door. "Something happened and it soured my entire feeling for the game. I couldn't get passionate about it anymore. I couldn't stand to be on the field. Every time a player comes in with a shredded ACL or a broken clavicle and a season's worth of closed head injuries, it makes my skin hurt. All sports are brutal but the toll football takes on the body is insane."

The noise inside the auditorium echoed and bounced as excited fans made their way from the entrance to their seats. I touched his elbow and Lando stopped and looked at me with lifted eyebrows. "So what happened?"

I saw his quick intake of breath and watched as he debated how to answer me. He was opening his mouth to reply when an arm was suddenly slung around my neck in a strangling hug and my torso was bent over as a big hand smacked across my abs.

"If it ain't super cop. Long time no see, Dom. We miss you around the station, dude. When you getting your lazy ass back to work?"

I grunted and straightened up to see a couple of my

fellow patrol officers dressed down and off duty, clearly here for the game as well. The one that had jumped me was Devin Shea and the other was his partner, Diego Ramirez. Both had been in the academy when Royal and I had been going through the paces and both had been there the night I got shot and fell. They were good guys, good cops, and part of the brotherhood I missed so much I could taste the bitterness of the loss on my tongue.

I rubbed my stomach like the smack had hurt worse than it did and gave the men a scowl. "I'm working on it. How about you take a header off a ten-story building and see how quickly you bounce back, hot shot." I narrowed my eyes playfully. "Dick."

He laughed and then got serious. "Heard about your girl and the accident. Sucks to have you both down for the count. We're short staffed as it is, and it isn't like the bad guys don't already outnumber us."

I hooked a thumb at Orlando, who was watching the exchange with a guarded expression and had taken a few steps away from my side. "Thanks to this guy and his magic, I'm hoping to be back before you know it. Devin, Diego, this is my physical therapist, Orlando Frederick."

The three men shook hands as Lando offered up a re-served hello. Devin's eyes widened and I thought he was going to make a smart-assed remark about me sleeping with the guy responsible for getting me back to work but instead he asked Lando if he was the guy that had handled the rehab of some professional snowboarder that I had never heard of. Lando nodded and before Devin could launch into fan-boy mode I grabbed my guy's hand

and dragged him towards the rink with a shouted good-bye over my shoulder.

I could feel the tension coiled tightly in the hand I held and I could see it on Lando's face. Something had just gone really wrong and we were in an arena with hundreds and hundreds of people, so I couldn't exactly ask him what was up. I made it to the first intermission between the first and second period with the Avs up by a point before practically dragging Lando out of his seat and back towards the parking lot.

He blustered and asked what in the hell was going on the entire way but I wanted to know the same thing, and inside the arena surrounded by strangers was no place to go digging inside of that complicated head of his. I stopped when we got back to the low-slung car and pushed him up against the side of it with a hand in the center of his chest. He was so startled that he finally stopped arguing and just stared at me.

"Okay, Lando, it's just you and me now. Why in the fuck did you go ice cold when I introduced you to the guys from the force? I know you don't like my job, I get that the idea of fixing me up so I can turn around and very possibly get broken again pisses you off, but those are good guys, friends. So what's the deal?"

His mouth opened and closed like he was a giant redheaded fish caught on a line. He put his hand over mine and moved it so that I could feel his heart beating through the heavy fabric of his coat. "You introduced me as your trainer. Not your friend, not your date . . . I wasn't sure what kind of role you were expecting me to play with the people in your real life, Dom. I was just being careful. I didn't want to give anyone the wrong impression."

I felt my eyebrows shoot up until they almost touched my hairline. I let out a deep breath and took a step closer so that we were almost touching. I put my other hand on his hip so that there was no doubt I was holding on to him, embracing him.

"All the people I work with know I'm gay, Lando. Every single one of them. I didn't hire out a sky writer and have the words 'I prefer dick over pussy' written across the sky, but I think the fact that my partner is the most beautiful girl in the entire world and there is zero sexual chemistry between the two of us is a pretty big hint. I'm not big on talking about my personal life at work because cops gossip like a bunch of girls, but everyone knows. Some are cool with it, some aren't, but I don't give two shits either way. I'm not embarrassed or concerned about who I am or who I choose to spend time with, and I would never ask you to be careful or be anything other than who you are when we're together. You're a good-looking guy, it's not a stretch for a couple of trained cops to figure out we were on a date and as for introducing you as my trainer . . ." I shrugged. "I want to get back to work and you have been key to making that happen. That's where my mind was at when I was talking to Devin. Nothing more or less." I shook my head and leaned forward so that I could rest my cheek against his. His skin was always so soft. Even when he was rocking a five-o'clock shadow the color of mahogany, it was still baby soft and silky against my skin.

"The only impression I care that anyone gets is that we are enjoying each other's company. We like one another. We are choosing to be together for as long as it lasts and that's it. If anyone else has anything else to say or think about the situation they can fuck off."

His hand rose up and wrapped around my wrist and before he blinked those wintery-looking eyes I could have sworn I saw a glimmer of emotion bright enough and hot enough to manifest into tears in that gaze. "I've never been with anyone like you, Dom." His words were a whisper that floated right into the center of my chest. A punch I could see coming and duck and maneuver to evade. Those light words carried by murmurs were sneaky and got inside of me too fast to evade.

I leaned forward so I could kiss him, so I could show him that I didn't care who or what or why just as long as it was me and him. He kissed me back, but it was softly, reverently. It was a kiss that said thank you for something I didn't even know that I did. I slid my hand over the sharp curve of his waist until I could reach his ass under the hem of his heavy coat. I gave the firm globe a playful squeeze and pulled back.

"I've never been with anyone like you either, Lando. You have a good heart, a soft center, but the parts that are hard that you protect like I might try to steal them away from you have some really sharp and ugly pieces to them. I don't know who made them that way but whoever it was wasn't worth it."

He put his hands on either side of my face and gave me a look that wrenched at my guts. I'd seen heartbreak before. I knew what it looked like because my mom had worn it ever since the day my dad died, and Royal had been colored with the same brush for the few months it took her and Asa to get on the same page about their relationship. That's what was on Lando's face as he gazed into my eyes. Pure, unfiltered heartbreak.

"He was worth everything, but he didn't think our relationship was and there is no going back to try and fix all the things that went wrong." He sighed and bent forward so that his lips skimmed the outer shell of my ear. "I hurt for a long time, too, Dom. I was a man that was nothing more than my injuries. I did my best to heal, but I didn't have anything that looked like a new normal until you showed up at my clinic. I want you to know that, however we end."

It was my turn to curl my hand around the back of his head and brush my fingers through his longer hair.

"How can things begin if you're already planning the ending? Doesn't seem fair."

His breath was warm and tingled the skin at the side of my neck. "You're right. It doesn't, so since the beginning is where things usually seem perfect and the ending is always tragic, why don't we just skip to the middle? There're good things in the middle."

It was his turn to run his hand over my chest until it came to rest over my heart.

Indeed . . . there were very good things in the middle and it was that center, that protected core that I think we were both trying to avoid and claim all at the same time.

Chapter Ten

Lando

I WOKE UP with a heavy arm wrapped around my chest and a thickly muscled thigh nestled between my own. All in all it wasn't a bad start to any morning, but the fact that I couldn't think of any other place that I wanted to be, that it was, in fact, the best way I had ever woken up, made alarm bells jangle in my head and had panic and unease slithering slippery and cold under my skin.

I saw it as clear as a bell last night when Dom talked to his cop buddies. Saw the longing, the anger, that they were doing what he couldn't do and I understood how much being a police officer really was tied to his identity. I knew he was going to get his job back. With him following his training regimen and finally letting his body heal in the correct way he was already 70 percent better than when he had first walked in my clinic door. His limp was almost gone and hardly noticeable anymore and though his shoulder was still tricky and too tight for him to use as his dominant hand, he was getting so good with his left side that it didn't seem to matter. He was going to be back on the force, back in the direct line of fire before I knew it, and I was going to be back in the position of caring for a man that cared for something more than a relationship with me. It was disheartening and as cozy as I was, all wrapped up in Dom's strong arms, I needed some space to get my head on straight.

I tried to slip out from under him and the covers without waking him up but as soon as I moved his eyes popped open and I was pinned in place by his earthy gaze.

"It's Sunday. Where are you off to?" I had taken him back to my apartment after the hockey game mostly because it was closer to the arena than his was and after his declaration that he would never ask me to be anything other than I was, I couldn't wait to get all over him. I was impatient. I was grateful. I was falling deeper and harder for this gruff cop I knew I was going to be able to hold on to indefinitely.

My escape plan had the major flaw in it that I couldn't just bail on him and leave him in my bed while I did so.

I shoved my hair out of my eyes and scratched my chest absently. "I have a family thing I try to get to once a month on Sunday. Since this is the last Sunday of the month, I figured I'd better make an appearance."

He lifted his arms up over his head and stretched, giving me a show of pure strength and masculinity as he did so. He ran a hand over his face and sat up so that the sheet that was barely covering him as it was fell all the way down around his waist.

"I should rally my sisters and swing by for a visit with my mom, too. I haven't seen much of her since I started training with you, and I'm sure she wants an update. I should go check on Royal, too. I need to make sure that pretty boy of hers is taking care of her the right way." There was a tinge of humor in his voice as he swung his legs over the edge of the bed and bent to pick up his jeans from where they had dropped the night before.

When he was all tucked away, he turned back to look at me where I was watching him over my shoulder. He was pulling his shirt on over his head when he told me, "For the record, when you need me gone, all you have to do is say so. My feelings aren't going to get hurt."

I stiffened and opened my mouth to argue, but the sharp glint in his eyes wouldn't let me. "It's not that I want you gone, Dom," I motioned a hand between the two of us. "This is intense and happening really fast when I just convinced myself it shouldn't happen at all. I'm just trying to catch up."

He put his hands on the mattress and bent forward so that he could give me a hard kiss. "Then say that. Don't make excuses."

I scowled as he made his way over to the yellow IKEA chair where he had thrown his jacket. "It's not an excuse. It really is a family thing." Not my blood family, but family nonetheless.

He fished his phone out of his pocket and took a minute to scan his notifications. When he looked up, he had his keys in his hands and a serious expression on his darkly handsome face.

"For the record, whatever we're doing isn't a race, so there is no need to keep up. We already decided we're in the middle, and if you feel like we're rushing, then that means eventually we're gonna hit the finish line. Keep that in mind, Lando."

Realizing he was dressed and ready to go, I pulled myself up off the bed and told him to give me a minute. I took a quick shower and threw on a pair of jeans and fitted gray sweater. I was never much of a T-shirt guy. Probably because I spent the majority of my youth and adulthood in a gym. I wanted my clothes to look like actual clothes and not stuff I could just as easily work out in. I scrubbed my teeth and combed my hair down and even though it all only took around twenty minutes Dom had obviously gotten bored and wandered off to check out the rest of my house. It was a cute little Venerable cottage I had paid more than I wanted to for in the Highland area of Denver, but the craftsmanship and flat-out love for the older home that the flipper had put into it couldn't be ignored. I snapped the gem up the day it went on the market and hadn't bothered to haggle.

My house had a lot less black than his did. I liked some color but I did have the requisite flat screen that covered the wall over the fireplace and a few signed jerseys that were matted and framed, that keep the space from looking anywhere close to overly styled.

Dom was standing in front of a wall that had a few pictures of my family on it and one of my favorite pictures of me and Remy from when we had first moved in together. We had our arms around each other, and Remy's best friend, Shaw, in all her adorable blond glory, was hugging us both. For a long time Shaw had been the only person in Remy's life that knew about me, that knew about us. The three of us looked happy, like nothing in the world would stop us from living the lives we were meant to live. How quickly that had all changed.

Dom tapped the picture and looked over his shoulder at me. "He's the football player in your office, too. Who is he?" I shouldn't be surprised by his keen perception. It was part of his job after all.

I found my own coat where I had abandoned it along with all my common sense in my rush to get him naked and to get myself inside of him last night.

"Someone that isn't in my life anymore." I hated talking about Remy, hated having to admit out loud that he was dead, that I would never see him again, that the world would never be touched by his beautiful and warm nature ever again.

Dom gave me a questioning look and followed me to the front door. "Not in your life but still on your wall and in your office? And if I had to guess, I would say the reason you no longer like football."

I bristled a little as we both slid into my car. The weather was steadily getting colder and I was going to have to swap out the sports car for my SUV in the next few months. I kept the big four-wheel drive stashed at my folks' until the weather really called for it, but I loved my Jag.

"He was someone that once was my whole world. Not anymore." It was so hard to say "because he died." The words always seemed to get stuck in my throat.

"So it ended badly but you cared about him enough to keep a reminder of him in plain sight wherever you look?" Dom was trying to put the pieces together, but he couldn't solve the puzzle when there were major pieces of it not even on the table.

I cut a look to Dom across the car that practically begged him to quit asking questions about this particular subject and about this particular man. "It ended as badly as anything can end and I never thought I would get over it."

He was quiet for the rest of the ride across town to his apartment. When I pulled up in front of it next to his truck, I heard him suck in a breath and then let it out slowly. "So did you?"

"Did I what?"

"Did you ever get over it?" He asked the question carefully like my answer could very well break apart this fragile thing we were building between us.

I rubbed my thumb over my lower lip and contemplated the truth. When someone you loved died, was taken tragically with no room for resolution or goodbye, it wasn't something you forgot or moved on from. The guilt stayed with you. The remorse covered you. The what-ifs buried you under mountains of possibilities but eventually you learned how to function with all of those anchors holding you down. Was I over Remy's death? No, and I never would be, but I had come to terms with my role in it and in his life. That had been a battle hard fought and I wouldn't ever take that progress or self-growth lightly.

"No, I'm not over it, but each day I work closer and closer to being okay with things I know won't ever change."

"The new normal?"

I nodded a little. "Yeah."

He had more questions and now some serious concerns. I could see them swirling and colliding in his eyes. But I didn't have the right words to soothe them away, so I leaned forward and gave him the same kind of kiss he landed on me this morning.

"I'll see you at the gym tomorrow. You're getting really close to your goal. You can probably schedule your physical with both your doctor and your job within the next month."

He just looked at me without saying anything and when he got out of the car he shut the door with more force than was necessary. He was upset and I didn't blame him, but I also couldn't tell him that he was angry about a dead man. That made me feel too exposed, too vulnerable, and where he was concerned, I had done a very good job of insulating myself from the start.

I tried to push it all to the back of my mind and focus on the twisty, winding mountain roads that lead out of downtown Denver and into the mountains towards the small, upscale community called Brookside. The Archers made it a point to have a family get-together every Sunday and ever since Shaw brought me into the fold I had a standing invitation to join them. I couldn't always make it considering work and my own family obligations, but I did try and stop by once a month just like I told Dom.

Rule and Shaw now had a baby boy named Ry and he looked so much like Remy that it took my breath away every time I held him. Remy's older brother Rome was also on his way to getting married and was expecting his second child with his pixie-sized girlfriend, Cora Lewis. They had a toddler, a tiny spitfire that was a carbon copy of her mother, named Remy . . . or RJ as the rest of the family called her. Not me. She was named after her uncle and her happy and mischievous personality would have thrilled him. I called her Remy and gave her hugs from both of us whenever I got to see her.

My boy was alive and well through memory and family. Spending time with the Archer brood always soothed the jagged parts of me that losing one of them had caused. We helped each other remember and heal. Remy would have danced a goddamn jig if he could've seen us all together and happy celebrating him the way we tended to do.

It was Rule that opened the door when I knocked and like I always did when I looked at him, I had to take a moment to remember he was not Remy. I had to soak in the colorful ink that covered his neck and hands. I had to zero in on the metal bars that dotted his eyebrow and the hoop that lived in the center of his bottom lip. He usually had some crazy-colored hair that was spiked up or shaved off, but ever since his little boy had been born he was leaving it the natural dark brown all the Archer boys were born with. It was longer than it had ever been and even had a little curl to it. If it wasn't for the cocksure grin and the sharpness in his blue eyes that were paler than my own, I would call him pretty. Rule had too much edge to be pretty, but he was close.

"You good, man?" It was the same every time I saw him. The same question and the same sad look in his eyes. I needed a minute and he gave it to me.

"I'm good." He reached out and clapped a hand on my shoulder and pulled me into the warm and welcoming house. It smelled like French toast and bacon. It felt like walking into a full body hug when I so desperately needed one.

As we walked up the stairs, I could hear Rome arguing with Cora over something and Shaw trying to play the peacekeeper. She was always trying to smooth things over, trying to make sure everyone was happy and getting along, sometimes at the expense of her own happiness. At least she had sacrificed that until Rule woke up and realized she was a beautiful young woman that had been in love with him for most of her life. I was hit at the knees by a preciously little girl with blond pigtails who immediately lifted her arms up and demanded to be picked up.

I hefted Remy into my arms and gave Shaw a one-armed hug as she made her way over to my side.

"I haz a friend." At least that's what I think she was trying to tell me but her words were caught between baby talk and being all the way clear. I nuzzled her neck until she squealed.

I looked at Shaw, who was watching her husband take

their son from Dale, the baby's grandfather, so the older Archer could go and set the table. If anyone had ever had their heart in their eyes, it was the woman next to me.

"Who's the friend, Remy?" She laughed at me and patted my cheeks with her palms.

"He haz twucks." She stuck out her tongue and proceeded to blow a raspberry right at the end of my nose. Cora groaned from across the room as the big, retired soldier made his way over to collect his handful of an offspring.

Rome took the squirming child from me and put a smacking kiss on her cheek. "It's a long story, but there is a five-year-old she now has her eye on and I don't think it has much to do with his trucks."

I laughed and followed him into the room. Margot and Dale Archer had had to do more work than any of us when it came to dealing with Remy's death. When their son passed away, the entire family's fractured and already thin ties had snapped. It always did my heart good to see them all together and working, always working and putting things back in the order they should be. Neither Archer brother wanted their kids to go without their grandparents, so it took constant effort from all sides.

I walked over to the couch where Cora had planted her very pregnant self and bent so I could kiss her on the forehead. "Looking good, prego."

She swatted me away with a playful scowl and rested a hand on her swollen belly. "I look like I swallowed a watermelon. This kid needs to make an appearance like today."

"Don't even say that." Rome barked the order from where he was getting his daughter settled at the table. "I have no desire to rush to some tiny mountain hospital because you're impatient."

She made a face and held out her hand so I could leverage her up to her feet. "I'll just have the baby in the woods. That's a thing now. I saw it on TV." There was a spark of trouble in her mismatched eyes that told me she would always love goading her gigantic other half. In fact, I was pretty sure it was her favorite pastime.

Rome grumbled something under his breath that immediately had Remy looking up at him and calling out, "Whaz a shithead?"

That had Margot gasping and Rule almost rolling on the floor with laughter. Rome looked equally horrified and proud of his daughter as Cora crossed her arms over her chest and lifted an eyebrow at her man.

"She's at that age where she absorbs everything. Way to corrupt her early, Big Guy." Rome had the grace to look sheepish and to tell Remy that what she was saying wasn't something nice to say to anyone. But it was clear the more he tried to correct her, the more interested the little girl was in repeating the word. It was adorable and hilarious to watch a man that had fought for his country, taken a bullet for the woman he loved, and that ran a bar catering to some unsavory characters, lose an argument to a little girl that barely reached his knee. When she got older, the big man was going to be in so much trouble, and the look on his scarred face said he knew.

When Shaw came back into the room from changing

little Ry we all finally sat down to eat. It was easy conversation, what everyone was up to with work, how school was going now that Shaw was back at it, what Cora and Rome needed for the baby, and how the wedding planning was going for them. I basked in the familiarity of it, in the comfort and safety of it all. Nothing here felt like I was getting leveled, taken to my knees and forced to face something I wasn't sure I was strong enough to handle. At least it was that way until Rome looked at me from across the table, sharp-eyed and knowing.

"So you took on Royal's partner? How's that been going for you?"

I almost dropped my fork, so I clenched my fingers around it tightly. "It's going. He has some pretty extensive damage, but he's getting where he needs to be for a medical release to head back to work."

Shaw reached out the hand that wasn't holding on to her sleeping baby and put it on my arm. "Saint mentioned that he's gay." She shrugged. "I've never asked Royal but if it came from Saint as tight as the two of them are, I bet it's solid information." She wiggled her eyebrows up and down. "Just in case you wanted to know."

I let my fork fall and sighed. "I know he's gay, Shaw."

Her mouth made a little O of surprise and I caught Rule's gaze over her head. I forced a grin at her. "We all have a secret handshake that we all know to identify each other with."

Her eyes got even bigger until Rule put a tattooed hand covered in ink and wearing a subtle wedding ring on the back of her neck and squeezed. "He's kidding. Lando has

the hots for the guy and felt him out. That's how he knows
he's up for some dick-on-dick action."

"Rule!" Margot barked out his name at the same time
Rome did. From across the table, Remy looked at us all
with wide, innocent eyes and started chanting, "Dick,
dick, dick."

Rome growled at his little brother, who was once
again laughing hysterically, but the women at the table
had their eyes locked on me.

"Do you like him? Royal's partner, I mean." Shaw's
tone was soft and a little sad. She loved Remy just as
fiercely as I did and I could see the idea of me moving on
was as jarring to her as it was to me, though I knew she
would never, ever begrudge me any kind of happiness.

"I do like him. A lot actually, but I don't know how
seriously involved I can be with someone that has such
a dangerous job." I shifted nervously in my seat. "I don't
think I can handle losing someone I care about again."

The mood at the table dipped and everyone was quiet
until Rome suddenly leaned forward and poked the end of
his fork in my direction. "That's bull . . ." His eyes darted
down to his daughter and then back up to me. "That's
a lame excuse to keep from putting yourself out there,
man. I got hurt at home and it had nothing to do with
my very dangerous job. Shaw got hurt and she's never so
much as killed a spider. Royal's laid up right now with
a busted wing because some kid was texting and driving . . . and Rem . . ." He shook his head sadly. "That was
an accident, too. Bad stuff happens sometimes and it happens to people we care about. You can't live life insulated

because you are scared of getting too close. Ask my idiot brother over there how well that worked out for him."

It was pretty much the same lecture my mom had given me about not letting the fear win, only given in a much more authoritarian and no-nonsense way.

Rule nodded in agreement and leaned over to kiss his wife on the temple. "I told myself I was happy, told myself I was fine. If I didn't let anyone in, then there was no chance of being hurt, but there also wasn't the chance of feeling all the good stuff that someone special can bring with them either. There was nobody to love, no one to push me to make me better. There was just me screwing everything up over and over again. That's a pretty lonely existence, dude, and one I know my brother wouldn't have wanted for you."

Those were some pretty big guns Rule was pulling out because we all knew all Remy had wanted was for me, for all of us, to have the best life we possibly could. That's why he was willing to give me up. He knew I needed someone that could be with me fully; that could love me out in the open without shame or regret or any kind of excuses. Someone like Dominic.

I groaned a little and gave him a hard look. "You play dirty."

Shaw laughed. "He does and it usually works."

Rome nodded and stabbed at something on his plate. "Seriously, when you're with someone that has a dangerous job you become the something that makes them remember to be extra careful while they're out there doing what they have to do. You give them a reason to stay hyper-focused and you remind them every day what they have to lose. You give them something to come home to and that matters." I was sure he was speaking from experience. He had spent a long time enlisted in the army and, I was sure, had seen a lot of young men eager to get back to their families stateside.

Was that enough? Remy hadn't loved me enough or himself enough to come out and be with me the way I needed him to be. It hadn't been enough. Could letting myself love Dom, going all in with him so that he had a reason to be extra careful, a motive to try and stay as safe as possible, be enough to hold us together?

I didn't have the answer, but I knew without a question that my doubt, my hesitation, and misgivings were absolutely strong enough and powerful enough to pull us apart if I let them.

Chapter Eleven

Dominic

NO ONE WOULD ever call me a romantic.

It wasn't in my nature to plan occasions or to try and capture a moment with someone else. I was too practical for any of that mushy stuff. Well, I was before a certain adorable ginger had invaded my life and most of my waking thoughts.

"What is all this?" Orlando's tone was soft and slightly startled as I opened the door and ushered him into my apartment.

All this was me needing a moment, needing an occasion and wanting to share that with a specific someone, him.

I had cleaned my place up, like really cleaned, not just tidied it up like I usually did when he was over. I also called my mom and asked her how to make her lasagna that I loved. I think she went into shock before telling me to just sit tight because she would just come over and walk me through it. I rarely cooked and I *never* cooked for someone else. Luckily my mother had been married to a cop long enough that she had pretty good powers of deduction. When she showed up she not only had groceries but everything I would need to make the tiny dining room table off my galley kitchen look presentable. I did not shop at IKEA so believe me when I say the area needed all the help I could give it.

Mom helped me make dinner and peppered me with questions about what was going on the entire time. I really wanted to tell Lando first since he was the reason for my good news, but I couldn't leave my mom hanging after how awesome she had been, so I told her that finally, after three months of endless work and hours and hours of training, the doctor had given me a clean bill of health to take back to the department.

I had my physical and training course with the department set up at the end of the week. I was back in fighting form, almost back to work and so excited and proud that I couldn't contain myself. I deserved a moment and I wanted to have it with the man responsible for getting me there so bad I could taste it.

When Lando came into the apartment, his eyes widened at the spread laid out before him. I asked him to come over for dinner, which usually meant takeout or heading somewhere to eat. The only time we ate in was when we were at his place and he cooked, so I wasn't shocked by his surprise.

"We're celebrating." So much so that I actually had on black slacks and a light green button-up shirt instead of my usual jeans and T-shirt. The last time I was this dressed up I had been at a fellow officer's funeral. It took a pretty serious occasion for me to put the jeans away.

He bent his head and let his lips touch mine softly as I pulled him in for a kiss. I hadn't shared with him the fact my doctor's appointment was today because I wasn't sure how I was going to react if the man told me I wasn't ready yet. I'd worked so hard, we had worked so hard, I wasn't sure that I could simply roll with any bad news without it being devastating. Luckily that wasn't the case and now here we were and I was ready to throw my arms around him and shower him with gratitude and affection.

"What are we celebrating, Dominic?" He sounded amused and a little bit confused.

I should tell him we were celebrating being here together. Things hadn't looked all that good for a few days after he unceremoniously kicked me out of his bed and ran. For all the talk of not hitting an end or coming to an inevitable finish line, it looked exactly like that's what we were doing.

My ego took a ding and hollered at me to focus on getting better, to concentrate on getting back to work. My heart tripped and felt like it had been used for a soccer ball, all while my brain calmly explained that things between Lando and I were indeed moving along fairly quickly and there were still a lot of unanswered questions between us about my future and apparently about his past. My common sense told me this was just another bump in the winding and eventually forked road we were currently navigating together. My brain was smart.

After a tense two days of silence and no contact, he called and asked to come over. When he showed up, there was a discernible shift in his demeanor. It was like he had made peace with something, but I wasn't even sure what the battle was about. We ate pizza, bullshitted about non-sense, pretended to watch a crazy reality show about a naked man and woman trying to survive with nothing in the jungle, and then we fucked wild and uninhibited on the couch until we were both exhausted. It felt strangely like make-up sex but as far as I knew we weren't arguing and neither one of us had anything to apologize for.

Ever since that night though, things had fallen into a fairly easy pattern. He worked, I went to therapy and trained. We spent the night together at either his place or mine and every morning I woke up wrapped around him. It was nice. It was addicting. It was terrifying because I didn't know how long it would last and I was having a really hard time remembering what life was like before he took up so much room and time inside of it. It used always to be about the law, about my job, now it was about Lando and what was going to happen next.

"Sit down and eat dinner and I'll tell you what we're celebrating." I gave him a little grin as he looked skeptically at the table and the food sitting on it. "My mom came by and helped me cook. I'm not going to poison you."

He ran a finger over the tablecloth and then turned and ran the same finger down the buttons on the front of my shirt. The light touch made my breath hitch and my pulse skip.

"You dressed up your place and yourself. Must be something pretty special we're celebrating." I cleared my throat and actually did the gentlemanly thing and pulled his chair out for him. I don't think I'd ever pulled a chair out for anyone before.

"Very special." I walked around the table and sat down across from him. I asked him if he wanted a glass of the red wine Mom had brought to go with dinner and I could see humor dancing in his eyes as he nodded. Luckily my mom was a smart woman because I didn't have anything close to a wine opener in my place and the bottle she left had a cap that screwed off. After sloshing the deep red liquid into a couple glasses, I sat back and we stared at each other for a long moment. Eventually, Lando lifted the glass to his lips and took a swing. When he put it back down on the table he leaned forward a little and asked, "You went to your physician today, didn't you?"

I balked a little and reached up to tug at the collar of my shirt. "I did. How did you know that?"

He waved a hand over the table and all the trappings. "This is all a pretty big hint. He cleared you to go back to work, didn't he?" I wanted there to be some kind of excitement, some kind of enthusiasm in his tone, but there wasn't. He sounded resigned and fatalistic instead.

"He did. But it's not like I just get to walk back in and ask for my gun and my shield and demand to be put back on a beat. I have to get cleared by the department shrink, and then I have to pass the department PT test and get requalified with my weapon. None of that is a cakewalk or a guaranteed pass. But this is a big step in the right direction. It's what we've been working towards from the start."

He picked up the wine and swirled it around in the glass. I could see him struggling to be as happy with my news as I was and it stabbed at somewhere soft and un-guarded in the center of my chest. I put my hands on the table and leaned a little bit forward. "You're not excited for me." I held up a hand when he opened his mouth to reply. "That wasn't a question, Lando, it was an observa-tion. I can see that you're not."

He swore under his breath and then leaned forward and copied my pose. "I'm happy for you, Dom. It's me I'm not happy for."

I narrowed my eyes at him and fought to keep my ir-ritation in check. "What's that supposed to mean?"

"It means this is the one time in my career I kind of resent that I'm so good at my job. I knew we would even-tually get here, but I guess I thought we would have more time."

More time? It had been three months. Three months of hard work, uncertainty, and endless amounts of doubt. For me, it felt like forever to reach this point.

"More time for what, Lando? More time to decide if I was worth the effort or not?" It burned and the image of the pretty boy hanging on his wall and apparently on to his heart taunted me from a really dark place I didn't even know I had.

"It's not about you, Dominic. It's about what you do

and if I'm enough a man to watch you walk out the door every day knowing you might not come back. It's always been there, but now it's right in my face, and I still don't have an answer."

I leaned back and rubbed both of my hands over my short hair in agitation. "I could walk out the front door tomorrow and get nailed by a drunk driver while walking on the sidewalk. I could trip and fall down the stairs when it's icy and break my neck. And yes, I could go to work one day and up on the wrong end of a bullet, but that happens to a lot of very innocent people that have nothing to do with being in law enforcement. Caring about someone else, being with them is a risk regardless of what they do to pay the bills. I get that you don't want to be hurt again, but that isn't a promise anyone can make and keep." I pinned him with a hard stare. "I care about you a lot, Orlando. More than I was planning on caring while I struggled to get my life back, but I'm willing to take a risk on you. So you have to be willing to do the same if we have any shot at making this work." I was beyond frustrated because I thought we had gotten past this point in our relationship but apparently not. We really were just stuck in the middle, not gaining any new ground or moving forward.

He matched my stare for a minute before getting up and coming around the table so that he was standing by my side. He reached out a hand and gently brushed the backs of his fingers over my cheek.

"I took a risk when I signed you on as a client because I was attracted to you the minute you walked in my door.

I took a risk when we started working together because I knew you were going to push too hard and had to learn that your body has limitations and isn't indestructible. I took a risk when I let things get personal because I haven't cared about anyone the way I care about you in a long time and I thought that part of my life and my heart would never function right again." His thumb caressed my bottom lip and he moved his hand so that he was cupping my clenched jaw in his palm. It was a tender gesture, but there was still a bitter hardness in his eyes that seemed to override it. "You have no idea how hard it has been for me to take those risks, Dom, to keep fear from winning."

I lifted a hand and curled it around his where it was resting on my face. I turned my head so that I could press a kiss to the center of his palm and then curled his fingers around it so that he was holding on to it. Maybe this was the moment we needed to have. Maybe this was the occasion that we needed to remember. Maybe this was the make it or break it point in us being together. The fork in the road was looming and no, it seemed there was no other choice but to pick which way to go . . . together or separately.

"I told you, easy is for chumps, hard is for champions. You got me here; you fixed me. Do you really think I'm going to go out there and try and undo all the work you put in? Do you think I'm going to be careless and foolhardy knowing the effect that would have on you? If anything, being with you, seeing how much you worry about not just my safety but the safety and well-being of everyone, makes me more determined to get back to work and do my job better and more aware. I don't want anyone to hurt either, Lando."

I stood up and the chair toppled over. Dinner was forgotten as we faced off, indecision and longing at war in the air between us. Fear and love were two powerhouse combatants and it was questionable which one was going to win.

Love took the first swing as we silently moved towards one another, lips colliding and hands grasping. Fear snuck in a sucker punch though, because even though he was there with me, his mouth on mine, his tongue tangling, twisting, and turning with desperation in my mouth, I could feel he was also removed. He was back in that safe place where tender hearts and fragile feelings were locked up so tight nothing, not even love, could fight its way through.

Love fired back though. It was there when he ripped open my shirt, sending buttons flying every which way across the small dining area. It was there when the kiss gentled, softened, and turned from something that was hungry and anxious into something that was satisfied and content. His long and tapered fingers landed over my heart and tapped out a beat, played a song that only he could hear and that changed its tune to something deeper and darker as he stepped closer to me.

Our pelvises touched through our clothes. Hard on hard. Anticipation rolling across more anticipation. Our breath mingled and love and fear combined into something that was equally bitter and sweet. I put my hands on his hips and tugged him even closer, so there was no room to run. I rubbed the straining front of my pants against the bulge decorating his and got a sucked-in breath and shaky hands smoothing over my chest as a reward.

We kissed again. This time smoother. This time softer. This time with love instead of fear on the tips of our tongues. His teeth sank into the bottom curve of my lip with a playful bite. I fired everything up to detonation levels inside of me. I pulled his shirt off with little finesse and the sole goal of getting my hands on those long, lean muscles that were everywhere I looked when he was naked. Every single freckle on his body knew the stroke of my tongue and the touch of my fingertips now. But it was still fun to connect them, to draw a line with my finger down, down and down ever further below his bellybutton and into the top of his pants. Those sexy little dots went all the way down to the base of his dick and a few rebellious ones even marked the taut skin of his shaft. Not gonna lie, those ones were my favorite and well on the way to making an appearance as I pulled open his pants to get them out of the way.

Fear was back in the quake of his voice when he muttered my name as he bent his head to brush his lips against the side of my neck. That was a favorite spot of mine, one that he often used to distract me. Clever boy. But not right now. Right now I was determined, focused, geared up, and intent on beating all the fear down. This wasn't a fight I was willing to lose.

I moved forward so I could put my lips on his skin.

I kissed his throat. I kissed his neck. I kissed his chest. I took a second to run my tongue over the flat of his nipple and was rewarded with it pebbling up and begging for more. I rolled my hand around his cock and took a moment to squeeze it. I always thrilled that his dick kicked into my hand ready and eager. There was never any hesitation there. I also loved that it was pale, smooth, long, and hard just like the man it was attached to.

He made a low noise in his throat as his hip involuntarily thrust into my touch. His eyes were anything but distant now. They burned bright blue and they were so intently focused on mine that I felt like he was going to meld us together with the heat in them. I was beyond okay with that.

"I like the way you touch me, Dom." His voice was smooth as silk as it wrapped around me while he went to work on the opening of my pants.

I lifted an eyebrow and felt my lips twist into a smirk. "Then you need to let me touch all of you, Lando." I wonder if he knew that I was talking about that carefully guarded heart of his.

My own dick made its grand entrance and wasted no time in begging for his attention. Luckily he was happy to give it all the consideration it deserved and I lost my breath and maybe a good chunk of my mind while I watched us simultaneously work each other over. Darker skin against light. Hard hands against smooth surfaces. The stretch and pull of tender flesh as it yielded and asked for more and more. Both cocks harder than they had ever been as they throbbed in time to the stimulation. I could

feel his heartbeat through the thick vein running under-
neath his erection and wondered if he could feel mine as
his fingers danced and skipped with practiced skill over
my rigid member.

There was no room for love or fear now, only space for
want and need.

We shared another soul-melting kiss. One that had
our stomachs touching and each of us scrambling to get
out of our clothes. My tiny little kitchen was going to
see a lot of firsts tonight, Mom's lasagna and a tablecloth
being the least exciting of them, apparently.

I went willingly when Lando silently urged me to turn
around even though it meant I had to let go of his dick
and I could tell that he was close to coming in my hand. I
braced my hands on the table a shoulder width apart and
let my head fall forward. Love was exhausted from the
fight and hung heavy around my neck.

Lando's hand traced up and down my spine a few
times, leaving bumps of anticipation and excitement in
its wake. He used his knee to spread my legs farther apart
and I didn't need to look over my shoulder when I heard a
ripping sound to know that he had found a condom from
either his wallet or mine and was suiting up. One of his
hands connected with my ass cheek in a sharp pop that
did have me scowling and turning to look at him over my
shoulder. God he was beautiful and fear was nowhere in
sight.

"What was that for?" I didn't mind a little slap and
tickle every now and then, but we were about to fuck
over the kitchen table and a long-cold dinner, that was

enough of an extreme for one interlude as far as I was concerned.

He pointed at his now latex-covered dick which he was pressing down with his thumb and then at my backside.

"You want to move this party into the bedroom or you want to rough it?" He lifted both his eyebrows at me and waited for my response.

Well shit. I was usually prepared for any situation, but sex over dinner was not one of them . . . hell, sex any-where but in the confines of my very comfortable bed-room wasn't really one of them. It wasn't like I kept a bottle of lube stashed in every drawer around the house.

"Uh, rough it." There was no way I was going to shift the momentum we had going and let fear rear its ugly head back up.

"You sure?" He was always the caretaker and that was love.

"I'm sure. Now get inside of me." Going rough and raw wasn't my favorite, but anything that got this man inside of me I could handle. I turned back around and waited for the slow burn, the stretch, the automatic tight-ening of muscles against the invasion . . . it never came. Instead, there was the warm and damp lap of a tongue, there was the gentle probing of something much smaller and far more flexible. He would never hurt me, not when it could be avoided with a little love and care even if the pain was only temporary and well worth it for what came after.

Suddenly one of his hands was on top of mine on the table, his strong chest was up against my back and his free hand was around my still aching cock moving up and down as he pressed into me.

"Easy has its place, Dom. Not everything all the time needs to be hard." It was a fair point, one that he made over and over as he started to slide in and out of me in an elegant rhythm that juxtaposed the rough and erratic way he was working my dick in his hand.

It was a lot of sensation, a lot of different kinds of touching happening, but my favorite was probably where his lips rested against my ear so I could hear every pant, every gasp, every sigh that was ripped out of him as my body pulled at him and squeezed him. If what he was doing between my legs and behind me wasn't enough to get me off, the sounds he was making in my ear would be. To me, that sounded a lot like love . . . not like fear at all.

It didn't take long for his whole body to tighten behind me or for mine to quake in response. When he came, he whispered my name. When I came, I shouted his so loudly that I was pretty sure the neighbors could hear it.

We stayed like that for a long minute. Breathing hard and trying to figure out who won the fight . . . fear or love. As soon as he pulled out of me and there was distance both physical and emotional between us, it kind of felt like a toss-up.

"Sorry, I ruined dinner." He sounded sheepish and unsure.

I snorted and surveyed the mess we had made of dinner and of each other. "You made up for it in spades but don't tell my mom what we ended up using her tablecloth for. I'm gonna tell her I stained it and tossed it in the trash."

He laughed and our eyes met. Love was there, bright and clear, but that dirty bastard fear was still hanging on for dear life in the background. It looked like the battle had been won, but the war continued to rage on.

[illegible faded text from bleed-through]

Chapter Twelve

Lando

IT WAS ALREADY a tough day before I even met with my first client. Today Dom was going in for his last physical test to get his badge back and even though he never asked, I could see in his eyes when he left my apartment that morning that he wanted me there. It was a victory we had worked towards together, but no matter how hard I tried, I just couldn't bring myself to celebrate with him and it hurt me to hurt him. I just couldn't do it. I couldn't even wish him good luck as I kissed him good-bye.

Not only was I disappointing Dom, which sucked, but I was also feeling slightly heartbroken for another, unrelated reason. My client for the morning was a little girl that was going to be confined to a wheelchair for the rest of her life because her younger brother had found their father's gun and accidentally discharged it right at her within close range. It was a heartbreaking case because she was so young, but also because every day she came to see me her mother came and brought the little brother.

They were obviously a family in crisis. The little girl tried so hard every day to go through the exercises I gave her so she could keep her upper body strength and her core strength intact, but the mother, instead of being encouraging and helpful, instead of praising her daughter's courage and strength, spent the session fighting back tears and casting hateful looks at the little boy, who couldn't be any more than five or six. He never spoke, never uttered a word, but he also never left his sister's side. It was obvious the mother blamed him for the accident and her daughter's condition. I wanted to ask her why she didn't put that anger and blame on the grown-ups in the house that were responsible for gun safety, but I didn't want to cause any more of a rift, and taking care of the girl was my priority.

But like always, I couldn't stand to see anyone in pain and hurting, so the following week during their session I asked the little boy to help me with some of the exercises. At first he balked because the mother told him to stay away from his sister, but when I cut her a look that indicated I was a hot second away from kicking her out of the room altogether, she changed her tune. I moved the little boy in front of the girl where she was sitting on the floor with her immobile legs in front of her and handed him a heavy length of rope.

"You ever play tug of war?" He looked up at me with serious, sad eyes and nodded. "Okay, well, that's what you're gonna do with your sister. She's gonna pull as hard as she can and I want to you pull back without moving, okay?" He nodded again. "Once she's back as far as she can go you help pull her back until she's sitting just like that."

It took a minute for the siblings to figure it out. She was obviously not pulling as hard as she could and the little boy was terrified of doing something wrong. The rope kept falling out of their hands and landing on the mat between them, but eventually that innate rivalry all siblings had kicked in and they started actually tugging and pulling the way I wanted them to. It only took a couple times of the brother yanking the little girl back up into a sitting position for them both to be laughing and having fun with it.

I crossed my arms over my chest and looked out of the corner of my eye at the mother. "He could be an instrumental part of her healing process. She's going to need help for the rest of her life, including when you and your husband are no longer around. Trying to take him away from her isn't going to help anything at all."

The mother put a hand to her throat. "I kicked my husband out. I told him over and over again I didn't want those guns in the house."

That didn't exactly absolve her entirely of the blame, but I couldn't say I faulted her. "She forgives him. There isn't any reason you shouldn't be able to. It was an accident, a tragic, avoidable accident, but now you have to move on from that. She needs her family . . . all of them."

"It's so hard to move on from something like this."

Her voice broke and she excused herself to get some water as I continued to watch the kids play.

The little girl wouldn't walk again and the little boy had played a hand in that, but to her, all she saw was her little brother. Maybe it was because she hadn't been jaded by life yet, maybe it was that she was just a sweet kid without a resentful bone in her body, or maybe it was that she was smarter, more self-aware at twelve than I was at twenty-six and realized nothing was going to change. She could hate her brother, blame him and hold him responsible, but that wouldn't help her walk. She could be bitter, angry, and curse everyone for landing her in that chair for the rest of her life, but again none of that would make her walk again. Her new normal wasn't something I would wish on my worst enemy, but the clarity, the resilience that she was showing to get back to living life, was something magically and particularly eye-opening.

Bad things happened, it was how we navigated the fallout afterward that really defined what our new normal would be. You could do it gracefully, generously, thoughtfully like this precious little girl, or you could do it sloppily, haphazardly, and blindly like I had done.

I lowered myself to the floor and told the little boy to go sit next to his sister and told them both to try and pull me over. They huffed and puffed and obviously didn't get anywhere until I gave in and let them both fall backwards. They collapsed in a fit of giggles until I pulled them back up.

"How would you guys like me to show you some

things you can do together at home, fun stuff like this that will help your sister out?"

The little boy looked at his sister and then down at the floor. "I hurt her. I'm not supposed to be too close to her anymore." He sounded heartbroken and it made my back teeth clench together. I was going to tell him it was okay, that when we hurt someone it was our job to try and make the hurt all better, but the little girl struggled to get her body that suddenly wouldn't follow her commands closer to him. The little boy fell into her outstretched arms and started crying.

I had to blink back a wash of tears myself as the little girl petted the top of his head and muttered soothingly, "It's okay, Sammy. It was an accident. You didn't hurt me on purpose."

Was that the key to moving forward? Understanding that someone that loved you, that you loved, could hurt you even though they didn't mean to, accepting it and moving on? For a long time, I struggled with guilt, with regret because I pushed Remy, laid down an ultimatum that was going to make our relationship crash and burn, but I was mad at him, too. Mad he left. Mad I had to put the ultimatum out there in the first place. Mad that when he died I had to suffer and grieve on my own because the rest of the people that loved and lost him didn't even know I existed. I took that anger out on myself, let my life spiral out of control and did things that justified those feelings of anger and guilt, but now . . . now I had a new normal with a good man staring me right in the face and I couldn't pull the trigger because I was scared.

I was scared of love, where this little girl, this hero, this exceptional human being, was embracing it and using it not only to heal herself but also her family. In the face of such courage, such warmth and delight, I knew there was no way I could continue to let fear and doubt win. I may have lost Remy, but I wouldn't trade any of our moments together for anything in the world. That brilliant discovery of first love, that sharp sting of first heartbreak, I wouldn't give any of it up, even knowing how badly it all would hurt in the end. The same went for my relationship with Dom. I wasn't willing to give him up. I knew it from the get-go that he was a keeper and I was holding on to him, but I'd done a piss-poor job of allowing myself to enjoy falling in love with him. Fear ruined everything and it had taken enough from me.

When the mother made her way back into the room, I had the little girl on the exercise ball and her brother holding her legs as she rolled forward and he pulled her back. She had her arms out like she was Superman even though she was supposed to be using them to pull herself forward. I saw the woman open her mouth to say something to her kids, but she changed her mind and looked at me instead.

"It's like how it was before. Like they are just playing around and can't even feel how tragic and horrific all of this is."

"Because to them it isn't tragic. She's still here. She still loves him and they will find a way to adapt. So will you if you are open to it." They still had a long way to go, but if they all followed the little girl's example they would make it there.

I was headed back to my office after running through some exercises I thought would be fun for the kids to do together during the week when I didn't see her, when one of the other therapists came and found me to tell me a cop was waiting for me in my office. I tried to keep the chill out of my blood because I knew Dom had his last test with the department today and had no doubts he would pass, but ice still slid through my veins.

When I pulled open the door, I was surprised to see the pretty redhead he had introduced me to at the bar standing by my bookshelves looking at the pictures. She was dressed in the standard police blues and should have looked dowdy and frumpy but didn't. The girl was a stone-cold knockout and even a stiff and basic uniform couldn't hide the fact.

"It's so weird to see pictures of the other brother. It's like looking at Rule if he was from an alternate universe."

"That's how I feel when I spend time with him, only he seems like an alternate Remy to me. To what do I owe the pleasure of this visit, Royal?" I walked over to my desk and took a seat behind it while motioning to the chairs across the way for her to take a seat in.

"Dom passed his department physical today. He's getting his badge back." She pinned me with dark brown eyes that looked like melted chocolate but held a hint of displeasure in the warmth.

"I knew he would. I was with a difficult case all afternoon. I spent more time than I normally would with her, so I haven't looked at my phone. I'm sure he sent a message with the news. I'll call him and tell him congratulations."

She didn't say anything for a minute, but she did tap her fingers on the top of the hat she had propped in her lap. "It's a big deal for him. He's been working really hard to get to this point."

I narrowed my eyes a little and felt a scowl settle on my features. "I know. I've been there every step of the way right next to him."

She blew out a breath and it made some of the dark red hair that curled across her forehead dance. My boy obviously had a thing for gingers.

"Then why weren't you there today for him?" It was a simple question, but the answer was complicated. To start, he hadn't asked me to be there, probably because he knew how hard it would be for me, but seeing the censure on his best friend's face made it clear that I had been selfish and handled things with him all wrong once again.

"I should've been. I fucked up. I keep fucking up with him."

"He's in love with you, ya know? He's never really cared about much beyond his shield except for me and his family, but today . . ." She shook her head and bit down on her lower lip. "It mattered that you weren't there. He should've been thrilled. He wasn't."

I swore again and leaned back in my chair until it squeaked in protest. I ran both of my hands over my face and sighed. "I just had a twelve-year-old show how shitty

I've been living my life the last few years. I should have been there for Dom but if I had been, I would've missed the moment that made me realize I need to get my head out of my ass. I'll fix this, Royal. I promise."

She nodded again and a lopsided smile crossed her face. She was a stunner, but she also had a really kind heart. I could feel it envelop me as she told me, "You can start by following me down to the Bar for an impromptu surprise celebration party. He was obviously bummed you weren't there and took off for home as soon as he was released from the test. I sent his little sister to drag him out so we can give him a proper congratulations. Some of his buddies from the force will be there and so will his family. I also rallied my people, so the Archers will be there as well. He deserves more than a phone call, Lando."

Guilt and shame slithered down the back of my neck. I put my hand to the shivering skin to try and stem the sensation. "He deserves everything. I'll be there. I just need to finish up a few files before I head out for the day. It seems like it's the day for inspiring women to hand me my ass."

She tossed her head back and laughed. "Glad to be of service. Ari won't get out of class for another hour, so you have some time. Bring him some flowers or balloons or something. That would be adorable." Her dark eyes twinkled.

"I'd bring him a six-pack of beer before flowers, but since this shindig is at a bar, I don't think that will fly."

She gave a wistful sigh as she climbed to her feet and situated her hat back on her head. "You love him, too. I'm so relieved. I was stressing out over all the ways to ruin your life if you didn't. I was going to ask Asa for help and that would have been bad news for all of us. My man has trouble down to an art form. I'll see you later."

She swept out of the room and I was left feeling properly chastised and impressed by her visit. It was easy to see why Dom was so fond of her.

I dug my cell out of the desk drawer I left it in when I was with clients and fired it up. I had a missed call from my brother and a text from my mom but nothing from Dom. It made my heart squeeze and that shiver of shame turn into a full-on quake of disgrace. I was turning this all around right now. I was living life and not letting fear keep me stuck in place and away from all the great things that I could be moving towards.

I hit Dom's number and groaned when it went to voice mail. After his deep voice finished with the greeting, I left a short and sweet message. "I hear we have reason to celebrate. I'm so proud of you, Dom. I can't wait to tell you in person."

I hung up and finished with the files I needed to keep updated for billing and insurance and then headed out to Rome's bar. It didn't even occur to me that I should be nervous that Royal had said Dom's family was going to be there and I would be meeting them for the first time. I started to sweat a little even though it was chilly out and bounced my keys up and down in my hand as I pulled the door open.

The bar was already pretty full. Familiar faces mixed with ones I had never seen but they all looked excited to be there and happy to be gathered together. There was plenty of police presence and I caught sight of an older woman with dark hair that had to be Dom's mom. When a younger woman with similar coloring and the same olive-green eyes as my guy appeared at her side, I knew I was looking at Dom's family. I was going to put my big-boy britches on and go introduce myself when I got side-tracked by a shoulder bump.

I looked over at Rule and involuntarily sucked in a breath like I always had to do with him.

"So your guy is going back to work. You work all that out up here?" He tapped a tattooed finger to the side of his head.

"Yeah, I mean not all the way, but I'm not going to walk away because of his job. I realized today how stupid that would be." I sighed. "I stayed with Rem when he didn't want to come clean about what was going on be-tween us, when that was a much better reason to leave."

Rule nodded and clapped a hand on my shoulder. "Rome and I were both so pissed when Shaw finally came clean about Rem. We felt betrayed, lied to, and since he was gone the only person that we could take it out on was her. She didn't deserve it and then I was pissed at him for being gone, so I couldn't be mad at the right person. Anger takes up a lot of space and if you let it, it'll push out all the other good things that are waiting to be felt."

He pointed across the big room to where his pretty blond wife was talking to another pretty blond woman. It took me a second to realize that I knew her, well, had met her. It was the lawyer with man problems from the gym, and if I had to guess, I would bet the source of those problems was the hunky guy with the beard that towered above the rest of the crowd and couldn't take his eyes off of her.

"I had to lose everything before I realized that I didn't want to be angry at him, I didn't want to be angry at all. I wanted to love him and remember how special he was. I wanted to cherish the time we had and not taint it by turning his absence into an excuse I used to be a dick to the people that cared about me. Don't lose anything, dude. And don't use what you had with my brother as an excuse not to love someone else. He would hate that."

I didn't have any words. All I could do was turn and take this tattooed, pierced replica of my first love into a hug that finally made me feel like I had permission to move on. It was okay to be mad that someone you loved hurt you unintentionally, as long as that's not all you were. The sentiment and the lessons might have been Rule's, but the kindness and understanding that I needed all of that felt like shadows of forgiveness and understanding from Remy. He hugged me back and just as I was about to thank him for setting me free, the door to the bar swung open and I heard Dom grumble, "I'm tired. It was a long-ass day and I don't care if you told Royal you would bring me out for a drink. You tricked me into leaving my apartment, Ari. Next time you tell me you need me to come change your tire I won't believe you."

A husky female voice barked back, "Stop being such a sourpuss. One drink won't hurt you, grouchy pants."

I looked over Rule's shoulder where I was still holding onto him and my eyes locked with Dom's. I saw him do a double-take, his eyes widening as he took in the crowd gathered to celebrate his accomplishment and then narrow into slits as Rule let go of me and took a step to my side. I took a step towards him as he took one back towards the open door, his eyes locked on Remy's twin. The twin that shared the face of the boy on my wall. The twin that he didn't know was the surviving one of the set because Remy was dead. My omission, my inability to talk about my first love, was about to smack me right across the face.

"Not so out of the picture after all, is he, Lando?" Dom's voice sounded like acid poured over rusty nails.

"No, Dom . . ." But the explanation came too late as he stormed back out the door, leaving a room of stunned faces staring after him and his adorable little sister looking like she wanted to take a carving knife to my balls.

"What the hell?" Rule snapped the question out as I rushed towards the door.

"He doesn't know Remy is dead. I never told him and I still have pictures up in my house of the two of us. I told him things ended badly. He doesn't know because I was too much of a coward to tell him." Panic made my words rushed and jumbled together.

"And we have the same face." Rule's voice was understanding as I nodded and continued to hurry towards the door, where I was stopped by Dom's sister who put her tiny hand on my arm as I hit the door.

"So far I am not a fan of you, Mr. Fancy-Pants. You hurt his feelings by not being there today and now you have him running away from his surprise party. Royal likes you and says you two are good together, but if you keep hurting my brother"—her eyes were narrowed and I noticed they were a much brighter, sharper green than Dom's—"I will hurt you."

I pulled out of her grip. "I'm gonna fix it. Just give me a chance." I was making a shit first impression on the people that mattered most to him, but as long as Dom would hear me out, I would worry about fixing that later. If I thought the fear of losing him to something violent and uncontrollable on the streets was bad, I was wrong. The fear of losing him because of my own stupidity, the idea that he could walk away because of my own failings and hang-ups passed fear and went straight into stone-cold terror.

I had to do what I did best. Fix something that seemed unfixable.

Chapter Thirteen

Dominic

WHEN I PASSED the conditioning test and the sergeant in charge of administering it shook my hand and told me I could get my badge back as early as next week, I thought I would be filled with so much accomplishment and joy that it would burst out of me. Instead, I shook the man's hand back and wondered why it all felt anticlimactic. I thought maybe it had to do with the fact there was no lanky ginger there to congratulate me or to appreciate how far we had come together. Maybe it had to do with the fact Royal had been there, with her new partner. Making it clear that I was going back to work but things were different . . . I was different. Maybe it had to do with the fact I ran the course with twenty other recruits, huffing and puffing alongside the new generation, the generation that didn't know how bad it could be out there on the streets, the generation that still had the same shiny idealism and drive that I started out with but had let slip and slide somewhere along the way.

Whatever it was, I just wanted to be alone for a minute and get my head out of the dark and cloudy place it had slipped into. I wanted a beer and some quiet, but I should've known my family wouldn't stand for that. I'd made such a big deal, such a fuss about going back to work that there was no way they were going to let me throw a pity party when a regular party was just as easy to throw together.

I knew Ari had something up her sleeve when she showed up at my apartment after class and told me she needed me to change her tire for her. First of all I had taught both my sisters how to change a tire on their own before either of them could drive, but because she was my little sister and I never told her no, I dutifully put on shoes and followed her out the door. I was a little surprised when she guided me towards the Bar, considering she wasn't even old enough to drink until I caught sight of Asa's Nova and Lando's Jag in the parking lot. Of course, Royal would have a hand in any celebration that was planned on my behalf and all she would've had to do was whisper to her boyfriend to clear out the bar for her so that she could have the perfect place to gather everybody.

I was grumbling about leaving the apartment when the door swung open and before I could fake being surprised and happy to see everyone, my gaze landed on the man I was in love with in the arms of the man he was obviously still in love with. There was always that divide, that distance that kept me from getting all the way to him, and the canyon between us stood there in all his tattooed and pierced glory. He sure looked a hell of a lot different than the clean-cut boy in the pictures, but there was no missing that wavy dark hair or those unusually tinted blue eyes.

I might have been indifferent after the physical, but I was anything but after seeing Lando cuddled up to the tattooed hottie. I wanted to hit something or break something and since the closest thing to me was my little sister, I decided I needed to make a hasty retreat. I backed out of the bar like it was on fire and bolted for my truck. Sure, it was the coward's way out and I had just turned tail and run in front of everyone that I had been trying for so long to convince I was still the same strong, unbreakable guy that I always was, proving what a lie it all was. I just needed to get away and some space to breathe.

Hands grabbed my shoulders from the back and I almost turned around swinging. I knew it was going to be Orlando and as much as I wanted to deck him, I wanted to love him even more, which meant I could never hurt him.

"I don't want to talk to you right now." I had my keys to the truck in my hand and stared at him numbly when he reached out and snatched them out of my grip.

"I know, but you need to let me explain some things to you, Dom. I fucked up."

I bit out a laugh and watched the way his eyebrows snapped down over his eyes. "Obviously, but don't worry,

Lando, our ending won't be disastrous . . . it'll just be an end." I was so pissed I could hardly see straight let alone the remorse and sorrow that lined every inch of his handsome face.

"Do you really think that if I was going to rekindle something with an old flame that I would be cruel enough to flaunt that in your face on your special day, Dom? Do you really think that little of me? I haven't spent these last few months telling you how much I don't want you to hurt or be hurt?"

There was so much sadness in his tone that it smothered some of the flames of rage that were licking across my skin. I narrowed my eyes at him. "You said he wasn't around anymore and you also told me he was everything at one point in your life. What did you expect my reaction to be, Lando? Even it was just a friendly hug, that's too much when you are obviously still hung up on the guy. I never had a shot."

He sighed and put my keys into his pocket. He combed both of his hands through his hair and then reached out to put them on my shoulders like he was holding me in place in case I decided I wanted to run again.

"That's not him, Dom. It's not the same guy." I was opening my mouth to snap that I had two functioning eyes in my face when he shook his head. "Twins. They were twins."

Were? I relaxed my stance a little and crossed my arms over my chest. We just stared at each other for a long moment until Lando sucked in a deep breath and let it out slowly. "Remy and Rule Archer. Rule, the guy inside, is the only surviving twin, Dom. Remy got in a car accident several years ago and was killed instantly. For a long time I thought it was all my fault."

I was trying to follow, but I still felt like I was missing big chunks of the picture. "Why didn't you just tell me that when I asked you about the picture? You deliberately let me believe it was a relationship that just ran its course and ended badly."

He let go of my shoulders and took a few steps away so that he could pace back and forth in front of me. "Because I never really dealt with Remy dying, Dom. I loved him . . . hard. He was my first everything and I was head over heels. I wanted forever and I only got a couple of years. When he died it broke something inside of me and I was never really interested in fixing it. I was going through the motions, thought I was doing things right, and then you show up and show me I'm doing everything wrong." He cracked out a bitter laugh and turned to look at me with his hands on his hips. "I told you when we first met that the body has its limits and you need to listen to them, well, so does the heart and I thought mine had reached it and then there you are and all of sudden everything seems limitless. It was scary, Dom. It is scary. I lost someone I loved and in that I lost myself, too. I didn't even realize it until I started falling in love with you."

They were pretty words and I wanted to believe them, and the man giving them to me, but I was still unsure and confused. "Why did you think his accident was your fault?" I understood how powerful a motivator guilt could be and was looking for a way inside his reasoning.

I watched it get really close to taking Royal down in its clutches but luckily she was a fighter and had fought back until Asa showed up to pull her all the way free. Guilt would go a long way in explaining why he was still so hung up on the man that had been his first love.

"Because we fought the night he died. We had been fighting a lot after we moved in together. It was supposed to be a huge step forward but ended up being a hundred steps back."

He scraped a hand over his face and I could see sadness and memories that went along with a light in his eyes. They were so pale they almost looked silver as he continued to look at me.

"Remy didn't tell anyone he was gay, not his brothers, not his parents, no one knew. He moved in with me and used his best friend, a gorgeous girl with a wonderful soul, as a smoke screen. He let everyone he loved think she was his girlfriend and that we were just roommates. We were together for years, Dom. I never met his family, he never met mine and didn't want to. At first I dealt with it because I loved him and I thought things would change. I convinced myself that love, like we had, was obvious and impossible to hide and keep in the shadows. I was wrong."

A noise escaped my throat even though I was trying my best to be impassive and listen to his story with my head and not my heart. But he was breaking, shattering right in front of me, and that stabbed right into my heart. He was shaking and it had nothing to do with the chill in the air and I could tell the iciness in his stare was going to melt soon and that tears would follow. I had seen many parts of Orlando since we started, whatever it was we had started, but this was him showing me his soul. Uncovered, unprotected, and out from behind the shield of fear he normally kept it behind. It was beautiful but also hard to look at.

"On the night he died it had been a bad day. I was getting ready to graduate from school and was looking at different teams I could intern with. I told him maybe it was a good idea to leave Denver, that maybe we should leave and go somewhere that no one knew us so we could be free to be who were. He freaked out and told me he would never leave his family, he would never leave Rule or Shaw."

The first tear fell but before I could stop myself, I leaned up on my tiptoes and kissed it off his cheek. His hand curled around the back of my head to hold me in place as he rubbed the smooth surface against the dark bristle that decorated my cheek.

"I told Remy that it was obvious to anyone with eyes that Shaw was in love with Rule and that he was breaking her heart by using her to fool his family and called him out for doing it on purpose. Everyone loved Remy. He was the golden child in the Archer family and I knew they would accept him regardless of who he loved, but he refused to see it. He told me I could move wherever I wanted, but he was staying put. I asked him why he didn't love me enough to be honest about who he was, who we were together." Lando's voice broke and caught in my ear and even though I was still mad at him I moved to put my arms around his waist so I could hold him while he got the rest of the heartbreaking tale out.

"He told me he loved me as much as he could, but he loved his family more so I had to take what he offered or leave it. God, Dom, I wanted to marry him, I wanted to have kids with him . . . do you know what his words did to me? Rule called in the middle of the argument and asked Rem for a ride. They were always dropping things and running off because the other needed something, so it wasn't anything out of the ordinary, but I was trying to fight for our future and he was more concerned about Rule."

No, I didn't know how that must have felt for him, but I could imagine it felt a lot like what had coursed through me when I saw him wrapped up in the other twin's arms. It felt like the whole world was ending and like you would never feel anything good again because of it. Whoever coined the phrase "Love hurts" nailed it. It had the ability to hurt worse than taking a bullet and falling off of a goddamn building to the concrete below.

"I told him that even if he couldn't love me like that I loved myself enough to know I deserved better than to be a secret and I told him Shaw deserved more than being his cover-up. I told him if he left, then I didn't want to see him again."

He was crying for real now. I could feel the liquid slip between where our faces were pressed together and all I could do was tighten my arms around his lean waist and hold on until the end.

"He told me he always thought I deserved better and left to go get Rule. I never saw him again and when Shaw called to tell me that he was dead I couldn't even go to the hospital or anything because his family had no idea who I was and I didn't want to out him after the fact, so I fell apart and no one was there to help pick up the pieces because I'd allowed myself to live a lie."

He pulled back and used the back of his hand to scrape at his face. He was paler than normal and his eyes looked like the center of a blizzard, they were so cold and remote.

"I went to his funeral alone. I grieved for him in all the worst ways possible because I felt like I pushed him out the door, like I wasn't good enough to make him stay. I was mad at myself, mad at him for everything, and even when I realized the only person suffering for my actions was me and I stopped trying to punish myself, I still didn't move on. I still have a hard time admitting he's gone and when I see Rule sometimes, for just a second, I think it's all been a big cosmic joke. But he is gone, there is no going back. It's hard to give so much of yourself to someone and then for them to tell you you're lacking. It's hard not to be enough for someone that you love more than anything. It's hard not to be more than fear." He sighed and shook his head. "I told you I fucked up and I mean it. I handled this thing between us wrong from the get-go, Dom, and my only excuse is I wasn't ready for you. I thought I was taking a risk by getting involved, but I lied. I kept so much from you, never tried to explain why getting in so deep with you terrified me. You never had all the information you needed to understand why I am the way I am and that isn't fair."

I shifted on my feet as I tried to decide what the best course of action was now. I mean the guy had just poured his heart out on the cracked pavement and I couldn't say I didn't understand why he had been so guarded with me up to this point. Everyone has baggage and he obviously had never unpacked and was still living out of his. It was my turn to sigh and put my hands on my hips.

"I think . . ." I was going to say that I thought the best idea would be for us to maybe take a few weeks and decide what we really wanted. I was going back to work and even though I cared a lot about him and really did want to be with him, I wasn't ready to give that up. It wasn't that he wasn't enough or that my job meant more, now they were equally important to me. But I still didn't know who I was if I wasn't a cop and I wasn't ready to find out the answer to that just yet.

Before the words left my tongue, he was right up against me so that we were chest to chest. He put his hands on either side of my face and dropped his head until our foreheads were touching and then he rubbed the tip of his nose against mine.

"Dom."

I blew out a breath and it made his lips twitch where they were a centimeter away from mine. "Lando?"

"You are more than the fear. You are more than any kind of stupid excuse I can come up with to keep myself from being absolutely head over heels for you. I'll worry about you every time you walk out the door regardless if you are going to work or to the grocery store because I am in love with you. I know it's going to take some work, but I have it on good authority that means it will be worth it because we earned it."

I'd never had anyone besides my family and Royal say those words to me before, and I was stunned that they had the power to level a grown man. I put my hands around his wrists and let his hammering pulse soothe me as I closed my eyes.

"I love you too, Orlando, and I will never hide that from anyone."

His eyebrows twitched and a tiny grin pulled at his mouth. "Yeah?"

I nodded, which made our foreheads bump into one another. "Yeah, and I'm sorry about Remy and overreacting in there. It felt like a sucker punch. It's been a shit day all around."

He winced and then leaned forwards so he could give me the lightest of kisses and pulled back. "I'm sorry for all of it. I should've been there for you today. I should've been there for you all along instead of letting you go it alone. If it makes you feel any better, your little sister threatened to unman me if I break your heart and I don't think it was an idle threat."

I chuckled and let him put his arm around my shoulders and guide me back towards the bar.

"Ari is a handful but mostly harmless." I cut him a look and reached out to wrap my arm around his waist and tugged him closer to me. "My family will love you because I love you. We just need to clear a few things up."

Again those light eyes became glinty with moisture. "Yeah?" This time when he asked it, I could hear all the questions he was scared to ask in it.

"Yeah, Lando." My response had all the answers in that one word. No hiding and no fear.

We weren't about a beginning, middle, or end because now that he was here with me without the fear and regret he had used as a barrier, we were endless and our hearts were indeed limitless when it came to the love we had for one another.

Chapter Fourteen

Lando

4 weeks later . . .

My new normal was better than my old normal had ever been.

There was still an adjustment here and there and the fear that something was going to happen to Dom while at he was work never really went away, but I trusted him to take care of himself as best he could and I trusted him to take care of the love we had between us by making smart choices and being extra careful. Still, there was a night he was late coming over and when he showed up, he had a vicious-looking black eye, a cut on his cheek, and a gash that was taped shut on his forehead. He brushed it off as a tussle with a suspect that got out of hand but the wounds, as superficial as they were, still sent me into full-on flight mode and I'd had a momentary freak-out, which meant I shut down and pulled away from him . . . well, I tried to. Because we were in this together, Dom came after me, bugged me, pulled at me until I came out of my safe place behind the fear and he refused to let me wallow in the mire of worry and doubt.

I'd managed to smooth things over with his family and he was right, they loved me because he loved me even if Ari did watch me with eagle eyes to make sure I watched my step with her brother. They were a tight-knit unit and there were no words to describe how warm and right it felt to be embraced by the people that loved the same man I did. I in turn took Dom home to my folks and spent the entire visit giving my mother warning looks as she kept dropping hints about a future wedding and the possibility of grandchildren. Dom took it all in stride and with good humor. When he mentioned his sisters, I could see the wheels in my mom's head as she told him to bring them by for a visit over the holidays. I knew instantly that she was thinking that Austin was still single and if this Voss could settle down one of her boys, maybe another could work miracles and give the other a reason to return home. With her fiery personality and dark good looks, Ari was right up my younger brother's alley, but I didn't tell Dom that because he was fiercely protective of his siblings and I doubted he wanted my playboy of a brother around either of the girls.

Dom was also making an effort to get to know the new people in Royal's life and had gone out of his way to make peace with Asa. The cop and the reformed criminal would never be best friends, but he had stopped glaring at the golden-haired southerner every time he walked into the room. I had also asked him to go with me to say a proper good-bye to Remy and felt my heart fill up with even more love for him when he readily agreed.

On a cold and snowy day, Dom and I drove to the small cemetery in the mountains where the first man I loved was laid to rest. I never got to grieve properly, never had the chance to share the pain of saying good-bye with the people that understood just how deeply the loss went, so I asked Rule and Shaw to meet us there as well as Rome and Cora. The six of us gathered around the snow-dusted grave and bid farewell to the young man that had in some way or another had a hand in bringing us all together. I had lost a boyfriend when he passed, but gained so many experiences and a plethora of amazing people because of him. I considered all of them Remy's last gift to me. His way of showing me that even though he couldn't love me the way I needed, the way I deserved, he had loved me in his own way.

Dom put his arm around me when I started to tear up as Rule bent down and tapped his knuckles on the top of the tombstone and rasped out, "Your boy done good, Rem. We all did pretty damn good and it's a fucking shame you aren't here to see it. We miss you."

There was some sniffling from the girls as Rome and Dom cleared their throats, which was pretty much the male equivalent of sniffling and that made me smile. It was the good-bye I needed all along and the good-bye Remy deserved from me. I was getting ready to tell the Archer boys and their woman how much I appreciated them doing this for me when Cora suddenly let out a little shriek that sounded extra sharp in the quiet of the cemetery. Rome looked down at her with a frown that made his scarred face look even fiercer than it normally did.

"What's wrong?" The tiny blond put a hand on her very big belly and blinked wide eyes up at the giant former soldier.

"Umm . . . don't panic, but I think we need to go . . . now!" She was always a bossy little thing, but in this circumstance everyone jumped to do her bidding.

A moment that was somber and heavy was suddenly filled with giddy excitement and chaotic joy. It was almost like there was some divine intervention, some guiding hand that decided the time to be sad was over, life was moving on, families were growing and everyone was exactly where they were supposed to be. Remy might not be there in the flesh to witness it, but there was something in the air, a little tingle at the back of my neck that reminded me those that we loved lived on in all of us.

It was a rush back down the mountain to get Cora to the hospital before the newest Archer made his appearance. Zowen Phillip Archer was as much a tiny replica of his big, badass father as any newborn could be. Everyone was happy and safe, resting comfortably and well loved.

Soon after the visit, Dom and I settled into each other's lives with very little hitch or hiccups. There were still new things about one another that we were discovering now that the distance and hesitation I had built between us was gone, but for the most part the time we spent together felt fated, it felt comfortable and well-worn. When we were together it was like love wrapped around us in a cozy blanket and for all his talk about working for it and appreciating the results of conquering something that was hard, being in love with each other was easy and really no struggle at all.

After my freak-out over his face when he was hurt I noticed Dom's attitude about his job started to change a little. For the first few weeks when he went back he left for every shift from either my house or his apartment with a loose smile and some pep in his step. After the incident that left him slightly roughed up and me practically inconsolable, I noticed when he left for his shift he did it with more trepidation and far less enthusiasm. I questioned him about it one night while we were getting ready for bed and he brushed me off saying that he was just having some trouble finding his groove with a new partner. I didn't believe it was that simple but as badly as he wanted his badge and his job back, I couldn't figure out what could be bothering him, since he had gotten everything he wanted . . . including me.

I let it drop for the time being but as the days went on, the more and more dissatisfied he got. He was withdrawn and sullen. He was quiet and moody. He was acting an awful lot like I did when I first realized I was falling for him, so I called him on it and was promptly shut down again.

That morning before we both left for work I handed Dom a cup of coffee and told him flatly, "You need to tell me what's going on with you. I can't be in a relationship where we keep things from one another, Dom. There's too much at stake here for you to start shutting me out now." I knew it was hypocritical considering I'd kept him in the dark for so long, but I knew now what we had to lose if he didn't let me in.

He narrowed his eyes at me over the rim of his coffee mug. "Everything is fine, Lando. I'm just trying to settle in."

I shook my head at him. "Things are not fine. You're not happy, Dom, and I can see it."

His dark eyebrows winged up and he turned to put his mug on the counter. "You make me happy. Coming home to you and going to bed with you every night is better than anything has ever been."

Well, that was something, but it wasn't enough. "You make me happy, too, but there has to be more to life than that. You worked so hard to get back to work. I thought you would be celebrating, not moping around."

He shrugged absently and moved to grab his coat and his keys. "I thought I would be celebrating, too. It hasn't worked out that way."

I followed him to the door and grabbed his arm as he was about to leave. He looked down at my fingers and then up at the concerned expression I knew was stamped all over my face. "There has to be a reason it hasn't worked out that way, Dom. I don't want you out there, drifting in a job as dangerous as yours is. That's a recipe for disaster."

He opened his mouth to argue, I could see the fight fire up in his eyes and I had flashbacks to the last time I disagreed with someone I loved right before they walked out the door. My panic must have been clear in my expression because I saw the battle go quiet as he continued to watch me and then he leaned forward and gave me a quick kiss before shouting over his shoulder, "Maybe you're right. Don't worry about me and I'll see you later."

Had we met? Of course I was going to worry about him and a few hours later, when I was in the middle of a session with a pro golfer with a wicked shoulder injury and one of the staff came and found me to tell me once again there was a cop waiting for me in my office, I almost passed out. All I could imagine was Royal or one of Dom's other coworkers there to tell me he was hurt, or worse.

I pawned my client off onto another therapist and hurried to the office and came to a standstill when I caught sight of my guy standing in front of the set of shelves that still had the picture of me and Remy on it but now sat next to a picture of me and Dom from his surprise party at the bar. We had our arms around one another and even from this distance I knew how happy we looked together.

"You scared the shit out of me." I closed the door and bent over and put my hands on my knees so I could catch the breath that had been sucked out of me by the chill of fear and the dash to the office.

Dom looked genuinely confused as he turned around and stared at me. "Why?"

I waved him off figuring he would just make light of my overreaction and straightened so I could make my way over to my desk. I propped my ass on the corner of it and let my eyes rove over him. He really did look exceptionally sexy in that uniform.

"I wasn't expecting you. Did you stop by for lunch? I

was with a client, but I found someone else to finish his session for me."

He came closer to where I was standing and took his hat off and flung it on the top of my desk. He rubbed his hands over his face and sighed. "No, I didn't come by for lunch. I came by because I want to talk to you."

"Oh yeah? About what?" I couldn't imagine what was so important that had taken him from work and brought him to me. I also couldn't keep the trepidation out of my voice when I asked him what was going on.

He grinned at me and it settled some of my nerves. "I told you not to worry about me, Mr. Fancy-Pants. I just needed to figure some things out at work and I wanted to run everything by you first."

I felt my eyebrows shoot up in surprise. "What's going on with work?"

He started to pace back and forth in front of me with a loose gait. "I haven't been happy at work; you were right about that."

I snorted. "Obviously."

He cut me a sideways look and kept moving. I was getting whiplash watching him, but I knew he needed to get whatever was bugging him off his chest, so I didn't bother asking him to stand still while we talked.

"I couldn't figure it out. Something was off after I finished all the requalification. I shoulda been doing back-flips, but all I wanted to do was drink a beer and sulk." He paused for a second and put his hands on his hips and looked down at the tips of his black boots. "I thought I just needed to get back in the rhythm of the streets, that I just had to find my groove again." He blinked as he looked up at me. "The groove is gone. The passion I had for my job is gone. Something's been missing, and I haven't been able to put my finger on what it is."

Now that was surprising. "What's changed?" I loved the idea of him not being in danger every day, but I didn't want him to give up something he loved because of me. I didn't want him to look back on his life and regret being with me or feel resentful that he had to give up something in exchange for my happiness.

He huffed out a breath and started pacing again. "I changed. For most of my adult life, all I've ever been is a cop. That is the skin I was most comfortable in; that was the title I brandished around whenever I felt like I needed to justify who I was as a man. I was scared to lose that, to have to be something other than a police officer because that is all I've ever been. I was telling you to take a risk and yet I was refusing to take one of my own."

I made a hum of agreement but said nothing as he continued to pace and talk.

"It started to occur to me recently that I've always been a lot of things that are more important and more impressive than being a cop. I'm a big brother. I'm a son. I'm a best friend. I'm a survivor." He stopped directly in front of me and his eyes locked on mine. "I'm a boyfriend."

I couldn't hold back the grin that teased my lips. "A great boyfriend."

He grinned back at me and it made my heart trip and my blood start to heat up. "I think I've been trying to play the role of a cop instead of actually being a cop since I've been back and you're right, that is a recipe for disaster."

"So what's the plan, Dom?" I knew him well enough to know he wouldn't be here practically jumping out of his skin if he didn't already have something up his sleeve.

He lifted his hand and rubbed the pad of his thumb over the curve of his bottom lip. The action pulled my attention there and I wanted to replace his thumb with my teeth. "I've spent the last month with a rookie partner, a kid fresh out of the academy and while I may be slightly jaded and less enthusiastic about keeping the peace, this kid reminded me what it was like to be new, to have that drive and passion. He also reminded me what it was like to be a clueless kid trying to figure out how to make it home each day when the bad guys outnumber us and are better armed. I am starting to think about another thing I've always been, something else that has always made me happy and fulfilled." He stopped in front of me and put a hand on the center of my chest. "I'm a good teacher, Lando. I taught my sisters how to ride bikes, I taught them how to change the oil in their cars, and most of my favorite memories of going through the academy myself are tied to helping Royal and the other cadets out."

I reached out my own hand and put it on his hip. He was missing the heavy black belt that held all of his gear, so I wasn't worried about putting my hands anywhere dangerous.

"I still want to be a cop. I want to be involved in the law and I want to make a difference. Eventually I want to work my way up to detective, but the need to pound the pavement and tangle with the bad guys isn't as strong as it was before I realized I had so many other things that defined the kind of man I am, a man that I know my dad would be proud of."

I tipped my chin down in a slight nod. "He would be proud of you. I sure am. So if you aren't on patrol but you stay on the force, what does that mean?"

He took a step closer and when he exhaled, his chest brushed against mine. It made desire start to churn thick and slow all throughout my body.

"I mean I'm putting in to transfer to a position at the academy. I understand the hunger, the drive that new cops have, and I think I can be more useful to my city fostering that and molding the new generations that will protect and serve than I will be running down drug dealers and arresting petty criminals. I've always wanted to make an impact. This allows me to do that."

He closed the gap between us and kissed one corner of my mouth and then the other. It was a light touch, so soft and delicate that if I hadn't been looking right at him I would have questioned whether it was real or not.

"It also lets me do something I love without having you look at me like your heart is breaking every time I walk out the door, because you are more than fear too, Orlando. We are worth taking risks and venturing into the unknown."

If he hadn't already stretched my heart out so that it was big enough for him to fit into, it might have burst at the sudden rush of emotion his words had surged through it.

"You know I'm going to kiss the shit out of you for that, right?" My voice was raspy and full of a thousand different emotions.

He chuckled as I moved forward to make good on my threat. "Be my guest. I like having the shit kissed out of me by you."

I was going to kiss him.

I was going to hold on to him.

I was going to get my hands inside of his police blues and on his dick.

I was going to put my mouth all over him and then turn around and let him put his mouth all over me.

In the future, I was going to move in with him. I was going to marry him. I was going to have kids with him.

But right now, I was going to love and be loved because Dom had taught me how when I forgot.

He was right, he *was* a good teacher . . . among many other things . . . all of them great . . . all of them mine.

Epilogue

MANY MONTHS, FIRST kisses, engagements, weddings and babies on down the line . . .

I'd had to invest in more than one pair of slacks and more than a handful of dress shirts over the last year. I refused to wear a tie still and I would die before putting on shoes that were shiny, but Lando was okay with my dressed-down, dressed-up style and I hadn't been kicked out of a wedding yet. In fact when spring rolled around the following year, I was walking my best friend down the aisle and handing her off to the southern charmer that had stolen her heart forever. I'll only admit to a select few that there may have been a tear or five when Royal asked me to do the honors. I told her of course I would do it, even if it meant I would have to wear a tux. It was an honor and I jokingly told her I could use the practice because both of my sisters were involved in pretty serious relationships and eventually it would fall on me to give them away.

It seemed like Lando and I were always off to an engagement party, a baby shower, or a wedding. Now that I had immersed myself in his life and the lives of the people Royal had found to be her family, there was more love and happiness floating around than anyone could shake a stick at.

Colorado is called the Centennial State and it fit in a different way than I think the old-timers intended. It seemed like there were a hundred ways to fall in love in Mile High city and all of them were just as majestic, imposing, and rocky as the mountains surrounding the area.

I was sitting on an uncomfortable plastic chair in the heart of the Botanical Gardens waiting for yet another wedding to start. I was fidgety and sweaty because Lando had nixed the black cargo shorts I wanted to wear and told me that I needed to put on slacks. I wasn't sure what I wore mattered to anyone, not with the bride standing under a beautiful floral arch dressed in an ivory gown with just a hint of lilac at the bottom. She was facing her big, tattooed husband to be and the smile on her face was radiant. Truthfully, I didn't think they needed any kind of vows to express how they felt about one another. It was there on their faces and the way no one else existed except for the two of them.

I'd never really been into boys with a lot of ink and edge, but I had to admit the more of these shindigs I attended, the more I saw the appeal. They all looked badass and no-nonsense, but the way they were with their women was something special, something that deserved to be appreciated and celebrated.

I jokingly tried to talk Lando into getting a sleeve or a piercing and thought my Mr. Fancy-Pants would blow me off. Much to my shock and delight, he showed up after work one day with a shiny barbell pierced right through the tip of his dick. It was my new favorite thing ever, at least it was now that it was healed and I could actually put it to good use. I loved that there were still things about being with him that were surprising.

The priest finally told the couple they could kiss and they did so to a chorus of fanfare and applause. They looked good together, maybe not like a matched set but more like a special kind of curio that you just knew you had to have to make your space feel like it belonged to you, like it was home.

Suddenly the precious little girl with wild blond ringlets dressed in a frilly lavender flower-girl dress ran to where an uncomfortable little boy was standing in his miniature tuxedo amidst several giant men dressed the same and planted a kiss smack on his surprised slackened mouth. Much to the little boy's credit, he didn't flinch or pull away from the fairy-like little girl. Instead, he seemed to give a resigned sigh and took her hand and guided her down the aisle as the music for the wedding party to exit started to play. Just like a tiny little gentleman. They were adorable. They stole the show and it was the perfect ending to a flawless ceremony. When life moved on like this, it was a charmed thing.

I was still chuckling at the kids under my breath when Lando turned to me and put a hand on my thigh. His pale eyes glowed like the forget-me-nots that surrounded us and his heart was shining there as clear as day.

"I'm so glad you are here with me."

My chuckle turned into a lump in my throat. He did that to me a lot.

Leveled me with the way he loved me.

"There's no other place I would rather be." And no other man I would want to be there with.

Sometimes, if you're lucky, you can find the kind of love that is *Built* to last . . . Sayer and Zeb's story, coming January 5, 2016 . . .

Lando and Dom's Playlist

I TAKE MY book playlists very seriously. So because I felt that there was no way for me to accurately capture the soundtrack that would fit the life of an adorable twenty-something gay man, I asked someone special to put this particular playlist together for me.

Yep, not only did I dedicate this book to Matt, I also asked him to give it a heartbeat with a soundtrack that would bring the boys to life. I then promptly aged myself by telling him I had never heard most of these songs but still trusted that he nailed the playlist for our boys.

So once again, thanks, Matt, for being awesome, sweet and adorable, for loving my books, for loving my boys, and for making sure Lady Gaga is on the list . . . I do love her and that was my one requirement when I handed this project off to him! ;)

Dom's Playlist

"All-American Boy" by Steve Grand
"I Won't Let You Go" by Adam Tyler
"Damaged" by TLC
"Will You Still Love Me Tomorrow? (2011)" by Amy Winehouse
"Indestructible" by Robyn
"Fall into Love" by Wrathschild
"Not a Bad Thing" by Justin Timberlake
"Sure Thing" by Miguel
"Like a Drug" by Adam Tyler
"You and I" by Lady Gaga
"STAY" by Steve Grand

Lando's Playlist

"The Beginning" by RuPaul
"One Last Time" by Ariana Grande
"Alive" by Krewella
"I Don't Have to Sleep to Dream" by Cher
"Unusual You" by Britney Spears
"If I Had You" by Adam Lambert
"Peacock" by Katy Perry
"Fuck U Better" by Neon Hitch
"Ready for Love (feat. Chloe Angelides)" by Felix Cartal

"When Love Takes Over (feat. Kelly Rowland)" by David
    Guetta
"What About Us (feat. Sean Paul) [The Buzz Junkie Radio
    Edit]" by The Saturdays
"Fashion of His Love" by Lady Gaga
"Everytime We Touch" by Cascada
"Super Bass" by Nicki Minaj
"Insomnia" by Craig David
"We Found Love (feat. Chris Harris)" by Rihanna
"We Got the World" by Icona Pop
"Do It Again" by Royksopp & Robyn
"Beautiful Now (feat. Jon Bellion)" by Zedd
"End of Time" by Beyonce
"Gypsy" by Lady Gaga

Acknowledgments

I WANT TO extend a special shout-out to Nyrae Dawn for inspiring me to write this story. She wrote an amazing book called *Rush* about two young men falling in love and fighting to be together and it was so beautiful and honest that I really wanted to push myself to see if I could do something like that. I'm not scared to tell all kinds of love stories but I don't think without the elegant and thoughtful way she showed how it could be done that I would've taken the leap.

I always knew Lando needed a happy ever after and that was the push I needed to make sure he got one. I'm so happy I gave him his story . . . I can't say enough how fun and exciting this book was to write. I hope everyone that asks about Remy and him getting his own book understands now why that isn't a story I will ever tell. I do happy endings and he gets one . . . just not in the traditional way. I think Remy's happy ever after is seeing everyone he loved, everyone he tried to protect . . . including Lando . . . happy and ending up exactly where they are supposed to be.

I adore my readers and being able to talk to them and connect with them is one of my favorite parts of the job. I have a private group on Facebook where we all hang out. If you are interested in joining the group feel free to go to:

https://www.facebook.com/groups/crownoverscrowd/

I do a lot of giveaways and we have a pretty good time in the Crowd. It's really a place where I can connect one on one with readers and it is always all about the love. Believe it or not there are safe places on the internet. ☺

All my readers— Thank you for being you. Thank you for being honest and willing to take a risk. Thank you for letting me do my thing even if you wish my thing was something else. You are the best in the land and I really do owe you everything.

To the blogger nation— Thank you for being badass. Thank you for loving books. Thanks for keeping shit real. Thanks for working so hard often with little reward. Thank you for being invested and interested. Thank you for being on the front lines, sometimes it gets bloody and brutal there but you never give up the fight . . . neither will I.

My professional team. Amanda, Jessie, Elle, Molly (the whole Harper crew) . . . all you kickass chicks in NYC that do what you do like no other, thanks. Thanks for putting up with me and believing in what I do . . . even if it never is quite the status quo. Your support and faith is humbling in a business that often feels like it can eat you up and spit you out. At the end of the day I never doubt really amazing things will happen when we put our heads together. Kelly Simmon, thanks for answering the Bat Signal whenever it lights up and being all the kinds of awesome you are. Thanks for being clever and quick and thanks for being my friend. Stacey Donaghy, thanks for being you . . . which is an awful like being me! Seriously, thank you for just getting *it* . . . whatever *it* may be at the time.

My inner circle, what would I do without you guys? Melissa, Ali, Debbie, Denise, Heather, Megan, Vilma, Jen Mc, and Stacey (are you ready for more of my sweet dance moves?) thanks for simply getting me and getting what I do. Thanks for your honesty and time . . . I know how valuable both those things are. It may have all started out business but it feels so far removed from that now and I can honestly say you ladies are some of the real, true rewards that have ended up crossing my path along this journey. I love all your faces and want to smother you in so much love. You make me better and there aren't enough words to thank you for that.

Thanks to the people that have crossed my path and make me happy every single day just by being them and by loving books the same way I do: Matt (huge-HUGE thanks to you on this one, buddy), Becky, Renee, Christine, Pamela, Stephanie, Damaris, Melissa, Pam, Teri, Dani, Ivette, Jo-Jo, Jessica, Jenn, Courtney, LJ, and Carolyn . . . this is for you. Please just stay awesome and full of all the great things this industry needs.

To all the authors that are so disgustingly talented

and so inordinately gracious with your time and gifts, thank you for being my inspirations and my friends. You are all brilliant and who you are as people as well as storytellers is unparalleled. This huge thanks and virtual hug goes out to Jen Armentrout, Jenn Foor, Jenn Cooksey, Jen McLaughlin, Tiffany King, Cora Carmack, Emma Hart, Renee Carlino, Nyrae Dawn, Kristy Bromberg, Katie McGerry, Adriane Leigh, Megan Erickson, Jamie Shaw, Tammara Webber, Penelope Douglas, Kristen Proby, Amy Jackson, Rebecca Shea, Laurelin Page, Ek Blair, SC Stephens, Molly McAdams, Crystal Perkins, Kimberly Knight, Tijan, Karina Halle, Christina Lauren, Chelsea M. Cameron, Sophie Jordan, Daisy Prescott, Michelle Valentine, Felicia Lynn, Harper Sloan, Aleatha Romig, Monica Murphy, Erin McCarthy, Liliana Hart, Laura Kaye, Heather Self and Kathleen Tucker. Seriously, I admire every author on this list and what they add to this business and to my writerly life. If you are looking for a solid book to read I promise they won't disappoint.

I can never thank my mom and dad enough for all the things they have done for me, or for the enormous amount of support they have shown since this writing gig took off. They are just the best of the best and no kid is luckier than me. Thanks, Mom and Dad, for being all the things . . . ALWAYS.

As always I love to holler at my best buddy Mike Maley because he's an awesome dude and he spends a lot of time taking care of things for me when I'm not around to do it. You're the best, Mike, and I don't know what I would do without you . . . at all!!

Last but not least, thanks to my furry little entourage for being my heart. Woof!

If you would like to contact me there are a bazillion places you can do so!

https://www.facebook.com/jay.crownover
https://www.facebook.com/AuthorJayCrownover?ref=hl
Follow me @jaycrownover on Twitter
Follow me @jay.crownover on Instagram
www.jaycrownover.com
You can email me at: JayCrownover@gmail.com
http://jaycrownover.blogspot.com/
https://www.goodreads.com/Crownover
http://www.donaghyliterary.com/jay-crownover.html
http://www.avonromance.com/author/jay-crownover

Keep reading for a sneak peek at the first full-length novel in bestselling author Jay Crownover's new heart-wrenching Saints of Denver series,

BUILT

Sayer Cole and Zeb Fuller couldn't be more different. She's country club and fine-dining, he's cellblock and sawdust. Sayer spends her days in litigation, while Zeb spends his working with his hands. She's French silk, he's all denim and flannel.

Zeb's wanted the stunning blonde since the moment he laid eyes on her. It doesn't matter how many smooth moves he makes, the reserved lawyer seems determinedly oblivious to his interest—either that or she doesn't return it. Sayer is certain the rough, hard, hot-as-hell Zeb could never want someone as closed off and restrained as she is, which is a shame because something tells her he might be the guy to finally melt her icy exterior.

But just as things start to heat up, Zeb is blindsided by a life-altering moment from his past. He needs Sayer's professional help to right a wrong and to save more than himself. He can't risk what's at stake just because his attraction to Sayer feels all consuming. But as these op-posites dig in for the fight of their lives, battling together to save a family, the steam created when fire and ice col-lide can no longer be ignored.

Available January 2016

Prologue

I MET HER at a bar.

She had a beer bottle in her hand even though she looked like she should be sipping champagne out of an expensive flute and that inexplicably turned me on. She was pretty and looked completely out of place in the no-name bar sitting across from one of my longtime friends who also happened to be her long lost brother. He was the reason she was here. In that split second that I laid my eyes on her I wanted to be the reason she stayed.

I knew it was rude and that the two of them needed some time together, some time to figure out what they were to each other now that she had blasted into his life unannounced. If I was a better friend I would have left them alone. As it was I made my way over to the tiny table and sat down. I was covered in sawdust and had drywall mud caked in the hair on my head and on my face, but she didn't flinch or bat an eyelash when I purposely broke up their party of two and placed myself as close to her as I could without actually touching her.

My buddy Rowdy St. James lifted his eyebrows at me as I stared at her while he introduced us. Sayer Cole. Even her name was elegant and sophisticated-sounding. She was an enigma, this pretty woman that seemed like she should be in anyplace but this bar with the two of us. She'd shown up out of the blue a couple of months ago claiming to be his half-sister, claiming that they shared a father, claiming that all she wanted was to be in his life and have some kind of family of her own. She looked too delicate to be that brave. Came across as way too proper to have said "fuck it all" and picked up her life to move it someplace unknown without being sure of her welcome. She looked like silk, but if my guess was right about her it was silk wrapped around steel.

Luckily Rowdy was a good guy. After the shock of discovering he wasn't alone in the world, and once he realized he had someone tied to him by blood forever and ever, he had warmed up to the idea of having a sister and appreciated that the sister was Sayer.

I liked Rowdy a lot. He was a stand-up guy and a good friend, but I had a feeling I was going to like his newly found big sister even more. In my usual tactless way I asked him without looking directly at the knock-out blonde, "So you have a sister? A hot, classy sister?" A sister that was also a lawyer so beautiful and smart.

I expected a giggle from her or an eye roll at the outlandish compliment, but what I got was a wide-eyed stare of disbelief as eyes bluer than anything I had ever seen on earth danced between me and her brother like she wasn't sure what to do with herself or with my overt interest in her.

I thought that I had gone too far, pushed the beautiful stranger too far out of her comfort zone. I was a big guy and knew I looked far wilder and rougher than I actually was. I figured it might be too much for a woman already obviously out of her element and depth to take.

Instead, Sayer surprised me and I could see by the way he stiffened that she surprised Rowdy too. While she wasn't exactly overflowing with welcome and warmth, she did ask me about the current project I was working on after Rowdy explained I was a general contractor and had rebuilt the new tattoo shop he worked in. She seemed genuinely interested, and when I told her that my specialty was rehabbing old houses and giving them new life, her eyes practically glowed at me. I wanted to touch her to see if she felt as smooth and polished as she looked. I wanted to leave streaks of dirt on her perfect face to mark the fact that I had touched her, that she had let me touch her. It was a primal and visceral reaction that I couldn't explain and I liked the way it felt. Liked the weight and heft of it in my blood even if I knew the feeling wasn't likely to be returned.

She told me all about a fantastic but crumbling Victorian she had purchased that was falling down around her. She asked me for a business card and I saw Rowdy stiffen across the table. I sighed and rubbed a hand over my already messy hair. I watched her eyes follow the light cloud of dust that escaped the strands. I was great at my job, loved what I did but I couldn't do anything with her or for her without laying everything on the line. Especially not with Rowdy giving me the death glare from just a few feet away.

I dug the card out of my wallet and when I handed it over our fingers touched. I saw her eyes widen and her lips part, just barely. She looked a little dazed when I grinned at her.

"You take that card, but understand that the man giving it to you has a past."

She blinked at me and cleared her throat. "What kind of past?"

It wasn't something I liked to tell a beautiful woman when I first met her. It was something I liked to work up to, liked to prove it was behind me, but with this one it seemed like I wouldn't get that chance.

"I tell everyone that I do any kind of work for or that considers hiring me on for a project that I have a criminal history. I spent time locked up for a few years and while I'm not proud of it I can't deny it happened. I was a hotheaded kid and it got me in trouble, but I'm the best at what I do, so I hope that doesn't discourage you from giving me a call." Hopefully for more than some construction.

Usually I got a concerned frown followed by a hundred questions about what had led me to serving time. I got none of that from the stunning blonde. She tilted her head to the side and considered me silently for a long moment before reaching down and slipping my card in her purse. If anything I could have sworn she was wearing a look of sympathy when she told me softly, "I see it every day from the inside. Sometimes the system simply gets it wrong." A slight grin turned her mouth up at the corners, and I wanted to lean over and kiss it. "People make mistakes. Hopefully they learn from them."

I don't know that "wrong" was accurate in my case so much as misguided, but the complete lack of judgment or censure coming from her made me want to pull her into my arms and hold on to her even more. I had made a mistake, a huge one, one that I was forever going to have to carry around with me, but I had learned from it, was still learning from it. That kind of understanding from a total stranger was so rare, especially coming from someone in the legal field. I wasn't accustomed to someone looking at me and seeing me, just me, not an ex-con loser, after I explained where I had been. It was wildly refreshing and attractive. I couldn't quite get a handle on what made the woman tick, but I would welcome any opportunity she gave me to figure it out. I found her outwardly flawless and pristine demeanor tempting to taint with my dirty hands and ways, and there was something about the way she watched me, the way she turned towards me like she was drawn to me that made me think maybe I wasn't alone in the inexplicable pull department.

Rowdy left and she stayed.

We had a couple more beers and talked some more about her house and what she wanted done with it. She already hired one contractor but felt like the guy was ripping her off. It happened a lot in the industry so I wouldn't be surprised if the guy was taking her for a ride.

Spending time with her was easy. She was fun to talk to and really fun to look at. I really wanted to get my hands on her house and of course on her, and I felt like she was maybe, kind of, slightly leaning in the same direction when I made the mistake of asking her about her past.

I asked about where she had been before she found out about Rowdy and decided to move to Denver so that she could get to know him. I was curious what kind of life she had where she could leave everything behind and not be missed. Really I wanted to know if she had a boyfriend or husband stashed somewhere, but the simple inquiry must have touched a nerve. The next thing I knew she had paid out the tab for both of us and disappeared into the night. She went from glowing and bright to frigid and untouchable in the span of a heartbeat.

I figured I blew my shot by being too blunt as always. I assumed she probably did have someone else in the picture and had been friendly and polite only because I was good friends with her brother. I thought I would never hear from her again and was baffled why the thought of that made my chest ache and my heart feel like it weighed two tons.

Imagine my surprise when she called me and hired me to renovate her house a week later without a bid, without a contract, without even knowing if I was half as good as I claimed to be.

Of course I accepted, but I knew once I was inside I would need to knock down and rearrange more than just the walls of the house, in order to get at something beautiful and lasting.

Chapter One

Sayer

6 months later

"Can't sleep?"

The soft question sent the glass of white wine I'd been chugging like it was cheap beer falling from my fingers and clattering noisily to the beautifully refinished hardwood floors under my bare feet.

The glass shattered and wine cascaded everywhere as I put a hand to my chest and looked over my shoulder at the pale ghost of the young woman I was currently sharing my newly renovated living space with. Her light brown eyes were huge in her face, and, like always, she looked like a delicate fawn ready to bolt at any noise or quick movement I might make.

I took a deep breath to calm myself down and gingerly picked myself out of the broken glass minefield so I could get a towel and the broom to clean up the mess. "Why aren't you asleep, Poppy?"

I knew the answer. The old Victorian I bought just a

few weeks after relocating to Denver was huge, had three different levels, was made of sturdy wood and had heavy, solid doors on each room. None of that was enough to keep the sounds of this young woman's screams of terror as she had nightmare after nightmare from reaching me. They weren't as frequent as when she first moved into my home. In fact they hardly ever pulled me from my own troubled dreams anymore, but every now and then I would hear her voice through the walls, hear heartbreaking sobs echoing across the rafters, and my brittle heart wanted to snap in two for her.

She pushed some of her long caramel-colored hair behind her ears and lifted an eyebrow at me. "Bad dream. How about you, Sayer? Why are you still up?"

I cleared my throat as I bent down to sweep the glass up.

It was late.

I was really tired.

I had a full day at work tomorrow and I needed to be up early enough so I could swing by the gym before I went into my office.

I had also agreed to have drinks with a fellow attorney after my final court appearance of the day. It was a semi date I had already rescheduled twice, so I couldn't reasonably back out again without looking like a complete jerk. Doing any of that on a few hours of sleep was less than ideal, but I was getting used to running on fumes lately. I too was having dreams that woke me up in the middle of the night, that left me shaken, heated, and too wound up to stay in bed.

Only my dreams weren't terror inducing—they were good. Oh so fucking good. They were better than good. They were the best dreams I had ever had. Hell, the dreams were better than any kind of actual sexual experience I had ever had while wide awake. They were the kind of dreams that had me jerking up from a dead sleep while I panted and sweated. I woke up twisting in my sheets and touching myself because the man that starred in each and every single one of them was nowhere around.

Control was everything to me, and Zeb Fuller made me want to lose it even when he was sound asleep in his own bed all the way across Denver.

I'd paid him a fortune to turn this broken down, sagging, sorry excuse for a house into a stately, soaring, and magnificent home, and so Zeb had his hands all over my real-life dreams, not just my naughty midnight ones. He had finished the last of the remodel a couple of weeks ago and ever since, I found myself missing the sounds of hammering, drilling, and the rumble of his deep voice. All the dirty, sexy things I secretly wanted him to do to me were chasing me into dreamland, making for rough mornings and some serious dark circles under my eyes. I was pale anyway, so there was no hiding the evidence of Zebulon Fuller's effect on me.

It was stupidly simple. I had a crush that I couldn't shake, and it terrified me.

It made me feel off-balance, unsure, and so damn sexually frustrated I wanted to pull out all of my long, blond hair by the roots just for a distraction.

I swore softly as a piece of glass slid across my fingertip when I bent down to usher the mess into the dustpan. I stuck the bleeding digit into my mouth and grunted in annoyance at myself. I had learned before I could walk that showing any kind of emotion was a weakness, a fatal flaw that would end with you in tears as the victor stood over your broken, weeping form with a look of pity and disgust on his face. I shouldn't have jumped when Poppy startled me. I was supposed to be honed of more glacial stuff than that. I didn't react to anything—ever. Poppy was still staring at me with wide-eyed curiosity so I pulled my finger out of my mouth and wiped it on the yoga pants I had worn to bed.

"I was having weird dreams, too. I thought a glass of wine would help put me back to sleep." My tone was frostier than I meant for it to be, but old habits were hard to break. It was habit and it was armor.

She shifted her weight a little and again I was reminded of a timid woodland creature always ready to flee from danger. She was so pretty, so delicate, and no one should have had to endure the things this young woman had been through in her short lifetime. Poppy Cruz was only a few years younger than my own twenty-eight, but when her amber eyes assessed me with a knowing that felt ancient, it seemed like she was eons ahead of me in both life and experience. Even though I had been raised by a father who was a tyrant, and had had to put my mother, who loved him and tried to please him right up until her last breath, in the ground before I was old enough to drive. My formative years had been spent trying to live up to standards I could never reach and mourning the loss of a woman I loved and loathed equally.

"You've had a lot of sleepless nights since Zeb finished all the work on the house. You seem . . . unsettled."

I wanted to roll my eyes in exasperation with myself but held it back. I shouldn't seem any way to anyone. My cracks were starting to show and that unnerved me to no end.

Was "unsettled" another word for horny enough to climb the walls? Because if so, then yes, I was most definitely unsettled. And ridiculous. I'd never had the mere thought of a man distract me or cost me much-needed shut-eye before. I was supposed to have more restraint than that.

I dumped the broken glass in an extra plastic shopping bag and then tossed it all into the trash. It took a few more minutes to wipe up the wine that was on the floor and that had splattered on the cabinets and bottom of the fridge.

"I guess I got used to living in the chaos of construction. Everything seems so neat and tidy now. So new. I'm sure I'll get used to it. This is my dream home, what I always wanted. I think maybe the fact I finally have it is still settling in. That's all." I had grown up in a home where what I wanted or needed wasn't permitted, so the fact that I had something that was just mine, that was tangible, solid and real, something that was untouched from the taint of the past still took my breath away when I thought about it.

I made sure everything was back to being spotless and

snatched a bottle of water out the fridge before turning back to Poppy, when she quietly said,

"I thought maybe you were missing having Zeb around. He's kind of hard to ignore."

He most assuredly was hard to ignore.

Tall, tattooed, and built like a guy who hauled heavy stuff around and swung a hammer like Thor should be, Zeb was impressive to say the least. But it went beyond the work-hardened muscles, low-slung tool belt and the flirty charm he liked to throw around so effortlessly. There was something rock steady and so certain that shined out of his dark green eyes when he looked at the world around him and the people in it. There was an inherent confidence and assuredness that poured off of him when he looked at a person, like he knew without a doubt whatever he was bringing to the table was a thousand times better than anyone else in the room. God, I could hardly handle how hot it was when he smiled and rubbed his hand over his neatly trimmed beard. Especially when that smile and a knowing smirk was directed right at me.

I had never been into beards, and I always thought I preferred a well-groomed, well-dressed man. A man who looked great in a suit and tie and knew all about expensive cologne and hair product in the proper amounts.

As it turned out, what really flipped the switch on my usually inactive libido was a guy who looked like he could cut down a tree with one swipe, had unruly dark brown hair that looked like it rarely saw a comb or brush let alone any type of product. It was a guy who made a sweaty T-shirt and torn jeans look like high fashion and that kept me awake all night long while I fantasized what those work-toughened hands would feel like sliding across my naked skin.

I didn't know what Zeb Fuller had done to me or to my common sense. All I knew was that he was keeping me up at night and making me resent every single time I turned icy and cold when he flirted with me. I hated that I couldn't act normal around him because all I wanted to do was rip his clothes off and climb all over him. I wasn't familiar with any of those emotions, so as a defense I locked them all down.

My awkwardness and ineptitude in the face of Zeb's overt masculinity meant that I could never find any words beyond polite pleasantries and clichéd platitudes, which, I had no doubt, gave him the impression that I was nothing more than a stuck-up bitch. I never intended to treat him like the hired help, but somehow that's exactly what I had done, and now the job was finished, Zeb was long gone, and I was having phantom orgasms simply thinking about having his hands and mouth on me while I tossed and turned in my very empty and very lonely bed.

So yeah, I missed having him around. I missed watching him, hearing him, and even smelling that unique scent that all men that worked hard for their money seemed to have. Sweat and accomplishment mixed in with something that just screamed hard work and sex appeal.

I pushed my long hair back over my shoulder and raised my eyebrows up at Poppy in a questioning expression similar to her own.

"You didn't seem to mind him roaming around the house while he was here," I said casually.

Poppy had had a horrible experience with her abusive ex-husband, and in the aftermath the beautiful young woman had shied away from all physical contact with the opposite sex, including my brother, with whom she had grown up. It was crippling and when I started work on the house I worried how Poppy was going to handle having so many strange men in and out of the place that had been her sanctuary since she started to recover from her abduction.

Initially she handled Zeb and his crew banging around the Victorian by never leaving her room. She spent all day locked in there with a dresser in front of the door until one night when I was supposed to get home early to look at paint samples with Zeb but was running late. When I finally got there, I was stunned to find the bearded giant and the fragile flower with their heads bent together while they looked at paint samples in my torn-apart kitchen. I was so stunned that when Zeb mentioned Poppy really liked an unusual shade of reddish orange for the walls I blindly agreed to the choice, even though neutral and serene was much more my personal style.

After the shocking splash of color made it onto the walls I was surprised at how much I loved it. It took me a few days beyond that to realize it was the same shade as a field of poppies, and then I loved it even more. When Zeb left, I tenderly prodded Poppy about how the big man had coaxed her out of her fortress.

It was simple really. He told her he needed a woman's

opinion. He wanted to make sure he was in the right wheelhouse and gave her the choice and the control. If I hadn't already wanted to kiss him, his simple understanding of how Poppy needed to take back the reins of her life would have made me want to jump him on the spot.

Zeb Fuller was a nice guy. Ugh . . . a nice guy I couldn't stop thinking about or picturing very naked. He had tattoos on either side of his neck and ones that peeked out of the collar of his shirt. He had ink that decorated the back of each hand and wild swirls and designs of it that covered every inch of both of his arms. I wanted to see what else marked his skin and then I wanted to drag my tongue across every single inch of it.

Poppy cleared her throat and walked over to get her own bottle of water out of the fridge. She leaned next to me on the island with its fancy marble top and sighed softly. Even the noises she made sounded like a fragile flower fighting to stay upright in the wind.

"I like Zeb. I was surprised that I did, but I really do. He reminds me of Rowdy and he didn't look at me like I was broken. Not once. Eventually I'm going to have to leave this house, go back to work, and I know that means I have to stop thinking every man out there is going to hurt me. Zeb is huge, I mean he's just so BIG, but nothing about him is threatening or scary once you get to know him. I think he was good practice for me, and I love how the kitchen turned out. I would've died if it ended up looking terrible considering it was the first decision I've made on my own in a really long time."

Rowdy was my younger brother who I didn't know existed until a year ago, when my father died leaving his secrets printed in black-and-white in his will. Rowdy had grown up in entirely different circumstances than my own, with Poppy and her older sister Salem. After some time and some tragedy, Rowdy and Salem had figured out they were always meant to be together, which meant he cared even more for Poppy and her current state of mind than he normally would. She was family, and now that I'd found Rowdy, and had dropped every part of my old life and moved halfway across the country to get to know him, so was I. My father's final stab in the back, his last cruel act of manipulation, had actually been the best and only gift he had ever given me.

I reached out an arm and wrapped it around her thin shoulders so I could give her a squeeze. Unlike her older sister, Poppy was missing any kind of curve or thickness on her frame. She was a waif and sometimes I thought she was going to disappear right before my eyes. I also wasn't terribly surprised when she wiggled out of my grip. She wasn't the biggest fan of touching even if it came from a safe place.

"I can call him back to . . . I don't know, I'll ask him to build a deck or a fence or something if you want more practice." I was only half kidding. I would love an excuse to have him back within ogling distance.

Poppy laughed and it was such a rare and precious sound it made my heart squeeze tight. I'd never had a roommate before, never shared my space with anyone so closely or had anyone else to give my time to aside from my clients. I cherished the time I had with this young woman so much that I often wondered if Poppy was healing more than just herself on her journey to take her life back. I refused to acknowledge the scars and wounds etched deep in my psyche and that festered all over my soul from growing up in the care of my father. But occasionally Poppy would say something, or reach out and touch me, or my little brother would call just to check up on me, and old injuries I purposely ignored would tingle as they fought to knit themselves together despite my persistent denial that they existed.

"No, but thank you for the offer. Rowdy calls me every Thursday night when Salem goes out with her girlfriends and asks me to have dinner with him. I always say no because I panic at the thought of being alone with him and going out in public around all those other people, but I think next time he asks I know can say yes. I can do this."

I nodded and tried not to seem overly excited. I didn't want to pressure her in any way. "That will make him very happy and I think it'll be good for both of you." I nudged her with my elbow. "And if you need me to get off work early or want me to come because it's overwhelming you, just say the word and I'll make it happen." Rowdy would understand if she needed me as a buffer. He always understood.

She gave me a tiny grin that looked like a baby bird trying to figure out how to fly for the first time, in its hesitancy.

"Thank you. That means a lot." She walked around the giant island and headed towards the room that was hers at the very back of the house and as far away from my master suite in the converted attic as it could get. She knew her screams of terror carried and had made it clear she wanted to be as unobtrusive as possible while she recuperated in my home. "Good night, Sayer. Sweet dreams."

There was a note of humor in her voice that made me think that maybe I hadn't been as coy about what—or rather whom—was keeping me up at night as I thought. I sighed and made my way up to my own room.

Zeb had transformed the abandoned and decrepit attic space in the house into a master retreat that anyone would love. It was modern but still had the vintage charm that came with an old house. The colors were all pale grays and soft blues. It was a place where I could shut out the rest of the world after a rough day in court or when I had a client and case I couldn't let go of. He made me a paradise in my own home and the only thing that would be even better was if he would strip and climb into the massive four-poster king-sized bed with me.

I called myself every kind of fool I could think of as I took in the tangled sheets and the pillows tossed in every direction. My imaginary Zeb got more of a reaction out of me and out of my body than my very real ex-fiancé ever had. I had been involved with Nathan for years and not once had he made my entire body quake, bow up, tremble from head to toe on the verge of an explosion that had every kind of sweet heat imaginable in it. That was why I had stayed in the relationship for as long as I did. There was no passion, no overwhelming rush of lust and desire that I wasn't equipped to deal with. Nathan was safe, easy, and I didn't have to pretend not to feel anything because I legitimately didn't feel anything other than a bland security that being with him offered.

There was nothing wrong with Nathan. He was kind. He had a good job. He looked good in a suit and liked all the same things I did . . . well, all the things I had convinced myself I liked up until my father died and my life turned upside down. And I truly believed that Nathan loved me even though I wasn't very emotive and worked way too much. He cared about me a lot even though we both knew I was never going to rock his world in the bedroom and that he was never going to be my top priority. It had taken the passing of my father and the discovery of my brother for me to realize that no matter how much effort Nathan put in and how accepting of my frosty personality he claimed to be, it was ultimately a relationship I didn't choose for myself. It was a relationship I chose to make my father happy and to keep him off of my back. I picked Nathan because that was what was expected of me.

I knew Nathan deserved better than someone that was only putting forth the bare minimum in order to keep the relationship alive, so despite his protest and his assurance that I was all he wanted, no matter what that looked like, I ended the engagement and packed up and moved to Colorado in search of a new life and a new family. I got both in spades and also a startling wake-up call, when a filthy, unapologetic and ruggedly handsome Zeb Fuller had sat down across from me at a tiny bar table while I was talking to Rowdy.

The way Zeb affected me was one of the main reasons I wasn't going to back out of my semi date I had arranged with Quaid Jackson tomorrow. Quaid was the kind of guy that seemed to like reserved blondes that were more comfortable in front of judges than they were between the sheets, and it didn't hurt a thing that he was also disgustingly handsome and over-the-top suave. The term lady-killer had been invented for guys like Quaid, and the way I felt around him, pleasant, warm but generally unaffected, was an emotional reaction I was familiar with. Quaid didn't make me panic or want to strip naked and throw myself at him. Quaid was safe.

He was a criminal defense attorney that had a legendary reputation in Denver. We had gotten to know each other when my firm handled his very messy and very public divorce not too long ago, so I was really hoping all he had in mind was a friendly get-together, because there was no way the man could be ready to jump into anything serious after that kind of train wreck. I was hoping time and attention from the handsome blond attorney would force my hormones to get their shit together and stop screaming Zeb's name. After tonight, I wasn't so sure it would work, but for the love of God, I needed to get some sleep and I was desperate.

I straightened out the bed, put the pillows back where they belonged, and hit the lights. I stared up at the ceiling and prayed the rest of the night would be Zeb free. Of course as soon as my eyelids got heavy and sleep began to beckon, I began to wonder what it was like to kiss a mouth that was hidden in a beard—which, of course, led to thoughts about what that facial hair would feel like as it rubbed against other parts of my body. My eyes popped open wide so I groaned and gave up. It was either a cold shower or battery-operated boyfriend time. Neither sounded as pleasurable as the thoughts that were keeping me up in the first place, but a girl had to do what she had to do and sadly I had been taking care of my own needs far too much lately.

Stupid, illogical crush. This was torture and the only solace I had was that in the past, I had always been too cold, too distant from my emotions to ever feel anything like this before. It was my first crush in my entire life and it was a doozy.